DEADLY PREMONITIONS

The Safeguard Series, Book Six

Kennedy Layne

DEADLY PREMONITIONS

Dedication

Jeffrey—Another happy ever after has been delivered. Thank you for giving me mine.

Cole—Your senior year is finally here. This only means the end of a chapter. Your story is just starting to unfold, so enjoy every minute of it and make great memories!

Veronica—Here's to wine and great friendships…and thank you for the suggestion of Safeguard's logo!

USA Today Bestselling Author Kennedy Layne brings the Safeguard Series to a stunning conclusion with your favorite characters that will have you staying wide awake until the very last page is turned...

The ominous knock on the front door in the middle of the night should have given Shailyn Doyle fair warning, but she answered it despite her palpable fear. Her past had finally come back to haunt her. It would be nothing more than her worst nightmares come to life.

Townes Calvert had been given a brief glimpse of nirvana before having it ripped from his grasp. He now has a chance to reclaim what was taken from him, but he must first hunt down the man responsible for murdering eighteen women and risk all that he loves.

Townes and Shailyn have no choice but to play a sadistic serial killer's twisted game in their search to reclaim the love they had once been forced to sacrifice. They both have envisioned what could be...but will they end up with nothing more than deadly premonitions?

CHAPTER ONE

*P*AIN UNLIKE ANYTHING *she'd ever experienced before radiated throughout her body. There were no tears. She couldn't manage a single teardrop. A deathlike chill had settled into her bones, chasing away all other bodily functions.*

She was paralyzed.

She was unable to move, to scream...or to hide.

She was at his mercy, of which he had none.

Shailyn Doyle gasped as her upper body came off the bed. She couldn't suck in enough oxygen. Her vision had become blurry. She would certainly die this time.

Panic took hold as its tentacles slithered around her soul, slowly strangling what life was left within her.

Shailyn wrapped her fingers around her throat in desperation. She struggled to draw air into her lungs to the point that even she could hear the whistling rattle of her frantic attempt at breathing. Seconds ticked by until the terrifying nightmare slowly fragmented into bits and pieces, eventually fading into dust as the terror disappeared.

"Two hours," Shailyn murmured to herself after glancing at the clock on her bedside table. The green illuminated numbers read three fourteen in the morning. "Progress."

Shailyn tossed the heavy comforter and sheet to the side in

acceptance. She wouldn't get any more sleep tonight. What was noteworthy was the fact that the top sheet was dry. She hadn't even broken a sweat in her throes of memories best forgotten. It was hard to be proud of that detail when she recognized her reaction for what it was—tolerance.

She swung her legs over the side of the bed. She recalled as a child always believing something or someone would reach out of the darkness and grab her ankles if she kept them dangling there long enough. She missed the days when the monsters had been nothing but a figment of her imagination.

Certain kinds of monsters were very real.

Shailyn automatically reached for the journal she kept on the bedside table, ignoring the slight tremor of her fingers. It was a byproduct of her time spent as a victim with a psychopath as her tormentor. She'd been left with a lot of daily reminders. That particular one didn't rate high on the scale of her insecurities.

It wasn't a conscious decision to write in her diary. It was a rote behavior after so many years of psychoanalysis. She didn't even think twice about sliding the pen off the soft brown leather cover and setting the black ink to paper. Her psychiatrist had explained that keeping detailed notes of her dreams and reactions could render the next night a little easier and maybe even less intense. That had never been the truth as she knew it, but it did give her purpose.

She wrote down every facet of her nightmare underneath her last entry almost twenty hours earlier. There was no need for her to turn on a light considering she never slept in the dark anymore. As a matter of fact, every lamp and overhead light in this one-bedroom house was currently shining bright to keep the obscure shadows at bay.

It gave her a false sense of security. The dark represented the evil that crept in with the night.

She honestly didn't care that the reassurance was a fabrication. The presence of the lights allowed her to physically walk through the rooms without hesitation.

Shailyn clipped the pen back onto the smooth jacket of her journal before setting both onto the nightstand. It didn't take her long to cross the room and carefully draw the heavy curtain aside. Her bedroom was located on the main floor of the house, facing toward the front where a heavily armored, black government-plated SUV had been parked ever since Shepherd Moss had escaped from a federal prison.

Shepherd Moss—her own private monster.

He was a very special demon summoned from the depths of hell itself.

He was out there somewhere, biding his time as he savored her soul. Shailyn didn't doubt that he was looking for her right this very moment.

After all, she was the only one who had ever gotten away.

Technically, that wasn't true. She had *not* been able to work her way out of the restraints Moss had her bound in for three days. An Arthurian hero had found her instead, and her shining knight had refused to let her die. She barely recalled him arriving as dark as the night. His armor had been as rough as sackcloth, moving among the shadows as if they held no sway over him. He was the antithesis of her tormenter.

What did astound her was that the torture she'd undergone had only lasted three days.

A mere seventy-two hours.

How was that even possible when her time spent in that hellhole had seemed like an eternity of several lifetimes? Of course, the same thing could almost be said for the years she'd been in the witness protection program. Now those three hundred and sixty-five day spans seemed endless, consisting of nothingness. Was she actually awaiting Moss' return with the promise of renewed torture?

She supposed she should be grateful. Eighteen women hadn't been as lucky as her, but then again, what was so fortunate about living this so-called life she'd been given?

Shailyn let the curtain fall back into place, checking to make sure that not even a sliver of darkness was visible before she crossed the bedroom floor in her bare feet. The coolness of the hardwood didn't bother her all that much, but wearing any type of shoe made her want to rip them off her feet and burn them. The scars on her ankles always became irritated when material rubbed against them for any period of time. She'd tried slip-ons in the past, as well as flip-flops, but those hadn't worked either due to the damage done to the heels of her feet.

It didn't take long for her to enter the living room and walk into the kitchen. The layout was simple, just as she liked it. The walls were devoid of pictures, there were no knick-knacks on the shelves or tabletops, and the few simple sticks of Ikea furniture had been rented with the house. It wasn't like anyone questioned the way she lived, especially considering she never had any guests. No one was permitted to enter her home, though she did make an exception now and then to the U.S. Marshals who had taken up guarding her night and day since Moss had escaped federal prison. Why make any friendships when she would most likely be relocated sooner rather than later?

Groceries were delivered to a drop box on her front porch from the local store. She had access to the small area from inside the house. She could lock the outside access door to the box before ever opening the inside hatch. The delivery service was a special arrangement the grocery store provided for the elderly and shut-ins.

The Marshals vetted the designated delivery man and all the

other employees of the friendly retailer. The grocery store tended to substitute their own brand a lot for other brand names, and they also charged a premium for nearly every item available through their service. Privacy apparently came with a price.

Shailyn hit the brew button, having already prepared the coffee maker three hours ago. She shivered slightly when condensation layered the sides of the glass carafe. Her feet were a little colder on the kitchen tile than they had been on the hardwood floor. The memory of a blue torch flame flashed across her mind's eye.

She crossed into the living room and looked over at the bay window to ensure the drapes were closed like she'd left them. Her need for solitude had nothing to do with the fact that she was wearing a pair of flannel pajamas.

Everything was as it should be. She didn't miss a step as she continued directly to the wall where her thermostat was positioned a little lower than eye level.

The digital numbers read seventy-two degrees. She didn't care what digits were displayed and intentionally pressed the up arrow twice. Heat from the furnace had a tendency to rise from the vents, keeping only the upper half of the room warm while leaving the floors far too cold for her sensitive feet. Winters in Maine tended to get rather brisk, and this house wasn't insulated properly. She honestly didn't mind her electricity bill being higher. She always kept to her budget. It wasn't like she spent her money on anything other than rent, utilities, and groceries.

She turned around to make her way back into the kitchen when the sight of her files on the desk caught her eye. The manila folder with ungraded essays sitting on top of the stack was crooked. She stopped walking, allowing her arms to drop to her sides, anticipating the assault.

Her heart stuttered in fear. Not because of death, but what came before it.

Everything on her desk had been perfect when she'd turned in for the couple hours of sleep she barely managed to obtain. She'd gotten into the habit of positioning items in a manner where only she would recognize if they'd been disturbed. And she was one hundred percent positive that the pile of school-work she'd been grading last night had been organized squarely in the left-hand corner. Not a millimeter had been out of place.

Okay. Ninety-nine percent sure, because one of the two U.S. Marshals sitting in the vehicle outside of her house had paid her a visit after noticing one of her two bulbs had burnt out on the porch. He had kindly replaced the lightbulb before rejoining his partner outside in the black sedan.

He could have easily bumped into the edge of her desk, causing the slight misalignment.

How many times had she overreacted over the years? Too many to count, that was for sure.

Shailyn bit her lip as she carefully looked over the living room for any other sign that someone other than the U.S. Marshal had been in her home. She cautiously put one foot in front of the other as she made her way through the entire house, eventually completing her search by returning to her desk after checking every room.

Nothing else was out of place.

"You're losing your mind, girl."

It was bound to happen, given the circumstances. She re-called a psychiatrist telling her that the average individual would have been institutionalized after suffering through the ordeal she'd been through. He couldn't seem to accept that she was nothing extraordinary. She'd switched shrinks after that, going through a long line of men and women who had various opinions on how she should handle her future.

Shailyn gently rested the palm of her right hand underneath her breast on the opposite side. She had been left with a reminder that she would never have a normal life…at least, not the way she'd once envisioned.

The rich aroma of coffee filled the air, prompting her to return to the kitchen. She did stop briefly at the living room window and verify that the ever-present black sedan was still in position. Two silhouettes were easily discernible.

She thought about taking them out a thermos full of coffee, but a couple of things prevented her from doing so. For one, she didn't go outside of these four walls any more than absolutely necessary. Two, she didn't even own a thermos.

Shailyn pulled a single brown mug that had seen better days from the cupboard. The eighties-style porcelain dishes came with the rental house, allowing her to travel light when she had to move. Honestly, everything she owned fit in one suitcase and an oversized purse. She was a simple woman, really, even taking her coffee black without any further additions.

She sighed in resignation as she took her steaming coffee into the living room, snatching up the folder of essays that had given her more of a jolt than the caffeine in her coffee could provide. She looked forward to doing some mundane reading from the writing assignments she'd given her students taking the online course she taught to pass the time. It was also a way to make some additional money, though her students knew her as Ms. Rachel Smith.

Her online persona, as detailed in the course curriculum, featured a picture of a random middle-aged spinster freshly returned to the farm after retiring from some teaching position. She sometimes wondered about the identity of the woman in the photograph, considering the lack of a full-fledged backstory.

WITSEC wasn't that original when it came to assigning new identifications to their patrons. Ms. Smith was a retired teacher from Iowa. That was the best they could come up with.

Thud. Thud. Thud.

The essays scattered onto the hardwood floor as the papers fell from her lap, taking the manila folder with them. Each essay was now drenched in coffee as she scrambled to her feet and spilled her hot beverage all over them. Her first thought was that Shepherd Moss wouldn't knock on her front door to gain entry. He would have just appeared behind her. Her second and most insightful deduction was that trouble had just landed on her front porch.

She quietly stepped over the wet papers and set down her coffee mug on the side table, not stopping until she reached her desk. One of those cheap buy-as-you-go cell phones purchased off the rack at the local drug store was tucked into the top drawer. She always made sure the device was charged and ready to go should she need to leave the property or contact the Marshals. It also came in handy when she needed to call 911…which had never happened in all the years she'd been in WITSEC.

Thud. Thud. Thud.

The knocking came again, only this time louder.

"Ms. Smith, it's Deputy U.S. Marshal Sturridge."

Sturridge was the Marshal who had changed her lightbulb a few hours ago, but she couldn't fathom why he would need to speak with her at this hour. She quickly opened the top desk drawer and retrieved her phone, pressing in the three numbers without initiating the call. She rested her thumb on the button as she slowly made her way to the door to evaluate the situation further.

"What seems to be the matter, Marshal?" Shailyn asked with

concern, but doing her best to keep her fear disguised. She tilted her head so that she could hear Sturridge's reply through the heavy door. She left off that this wasn't their usual procedure. Technically, the average WITSEC individual didn't have two Marshals sitting outside of his or her home on a regular basis. They were all given new identities and then expected to adapt, as if their lives hadn't been ripped out from underneath them in the most violent way imaginable. "Is everything okay?"

"Ms. Smith, there's been a development. We need to take you down to the Bureau's Portland Field Office as soon as possible."

Shailyn swallowed back the lump of alarm that formed in her throat. Had Moss killed someone else she'd known in her childhood? He'd done that exact thing a couple of months ago, most likely trying to draw her out from under the concealment of her WITSEC identity. The U.S. Marshals Service had been very adamant that she follow their instructions down to the exact letter since Moss had escaped federal custody. She'd complied, but she wasn't so sure she could continue to do so should he target her friends or family again.

Shailyn rested her forehead against the hard surface of the door and pretended for just a moment that this night was like any other. She'd get close to a couple hours of sleep, work for a couple more on the computer, and then maybe get a half hour rest before her day started with her schedule of online classes. The visual gave her the composure she needed before releasing all three security locks they had installed upon moving her into this house.

"My family?" Shailyn asked hesitantly after opening the door. Sturridge gave her an encouraging smile, though sadness was visible in his soft, brown eyes. He reminded her of those gentle cowboy giants Louis L'Amour had written about when her father had been a young man. She recalled her dad reading her books of the Wild West when she'd been younger, allowing them both to enjoy her bedtime stories. Sometimes she wondered if her father would have preferred a boy. "Are they okay?"

"Yes, ma'am, they're all fine as far as I'm aware."

"Then why am I needed at the Portland Field Office in the middle of the night?" Shailyn had once been the spontaneous type, living every second of every day like it was her last when she'd been younger. That day had arrived sooner rather than later, changing her outlook on the simplest of pleasures. "Am I being relocated again?"

"Ms. Smith, you—"

"Please." The word was just short of a plea. She was only human, and a flawed one at that. "Just tell me."

"Shepherd Moss killed an agent on the case yesterday."

Shailyn wasn't surprised. At least, she shouldn't have been surprised. Her breathing faltered, though. Moss had targeted someone else, someone unrelated to her. She suspected that it wasn't with no strings attached. She shouldn't feel any guilt over the man's predilection for torturing and killing people, particularly women. She'd done her part by sitting on that witness stand and testifying—no, reliving—every painful cut he'd sliced into her body. That included every burn he branded into her flesh, as well.

"I still don't understand what that has to do with me, Marshal."

Shailyn's mouth had gone dry and she couldn't even lick her lips to get the words out smoothly. Sturridge was glancing at his watch, as if they should be in a rush to get to the Portland Field Office. Since when had her activities ever been on such a tight timetable?

"Ms. Smith, the agent who was murdered had been assigned

to watch over a woman by the name of Brettany Lambert. She was a childhood friend of yours, correct?"

Yes. Brett had been Shailyn's best friend through elementary and middle school. A memory of them turning up the dial on her old boom box came to mind, along with a made-up game that kept them busy for hours. The first lyric to come through the speaker was what the boy she liked at the time was thinking of her at that very moment. They would each take turns, giggling their weekends away.

"Ms. Smith?"

Shailyn cleared her throat before nodding her agreement. She would go with Sturridge to the Portland Field Office, believing one hundred percent that she would be on a plane by noon. The U.S. Marshals and the FBI had been very cautious. It was their job to ensure her safety from the monster she'd helped put away. There had only ever been one man who'd truly given her that precious sense of security, and she hadn't seen him once since the day she entered WITSEC.

This was her life now…being alone with only a suitcase to her name. She often wondered when the hand underneath the bed would finally grab her ankles and pull her into the shadows. What if she were to go into that hiding place voluntarily? Was that how she would find her freedom? Was death her only escape?

Or could she slay the monster before he was able to kill her?

HE CLOSED HIS eyes, reliving every second he spent in the company of Shailyn Doyle. Her unblemished flesh had been a canvas from which he had created something beautiful. He did design his masterpiece on her body, but only she had the pleasure of seeing his work every single day in the mirror.

He wanted her back.

He needed to finish the seminal work he'd begun.

Did the authorities not understand that he was the one in control? Had he not proven his dominance time and time again? His parting gift in Colorado he'd left for Townes Calvert should have gotten his message across.

Townes Calvert.

The only adversary who had ever lived up to his most exacting standards. The man's personal interest in Shailyn Doyle would only make this game that much sweeter in the end. They would meet again soon, but he wasn't ready to see his entertainment come to an end. He preferred the long game.

He rocked back on the wooden porch and listened to the crickets and frogs communicate in their harmonious languages. Mother Nature could end their conversations with a mere slap of her hand.

He recalled the enchanting screams that fell from Shailyn's chapped lips—now that was his favorite melody.

CHAPTER TWO

"IT'S TIME. YOU need to bring the team into the fold. They'll all understand."

Townes didn't bother to take his gaze off the glass door that would reveal a woman he hadn't seen in years. He wondered if he truly had himself fooled in that he could look away if he wanted. He tried to convince himself that the larger part of his inner self wished this moment had never arrived. The smallest piece remaining of his soul was desperate to quench his thirst, like a man in the desert drawn to the mirage of an oasis. He'd come to realize over the years that a woman held a lot of power over a man's desires—his drive to be loved by her.

"And what exactly will they all understand, Sawyer?"

Townes flicked his gaze to the standard Federal Bureau of Prisons-made clock with its black and white dial and brown outer case that every military and federal field office seemed to have hanging on their walls. The seconds were ticking by too slowly for his liking. He loosened his tie while remaining near the large windowpane of the conference room, grateful that this location gave him a better vantage point for her arrival—the one alternative he had tried to avoid with his every action during this case up till now.

"You did what you had to do. It's something that each of us

would have done given the same circumstances," Sawyer stated, rubbing a hand over his face in exhaustion. "At this point, I don't believe any experienced investigator would criticize the choices you made back then."

"I planted evidence on a man so that he would be convicted of murder."

"You served justice."

"I played God, and now the bill has come due." Townes wasn't a man to sugarcoat matters, especially ones of this type of significance. He also wasn't one to make excuses. "I have to live with the choices I made. No one else needs to carry the burden for my actions, except the one animal who was convicted."

"And what if the time comes when your men—one of those experienced investigators—makes a choice similar to the one you faced all those years ago? What then?"

"They'll do the jobs I hired them to do, Sawyer."

Townes had rendered a personal choice that only a few men were ever in the position to make, though that list was about to expand. He would share his burden with this team, each of them having to swallow their share of the lie that had driven this particular serial killer. The time had come when it was no longer feasible to keep them in the dark. His motive was important for them to understand, though. He only harbored one regret for his sin—that he hadn't killed Shepherd Moss at that moment in time when he'd had the chance.

If he'd only applied four and a half pounds of pressure on that trigger so many years ago. Numerous people would still be alive and breathing had he acted, not to mention the most recent female victim of Moss' telltale methods. The agent he'd hired to cover for Coen hadn't deserved the fate she'd been delivered.

"Please connect Brody in on this meeting via secure satellite video conference." Townes couldn't wait all night for that glass door to open. It was time to get started. "It shouldn't be long before Deputy U.S. Marshal Sturridge arrives with Ms. Doyle, and I want everyone in place. I'd like to go over our itinerary one more time by the numbers."

Townes stepped away from the large windowpane. The shift in movement allowed him to catch the reflections of his team. They were all gathered around the conference room table, gearing up for a protection detail unlike any they'd ever participated in during the course of their careers. Each of them had completed dozens of VIP security details in their time, but none of them had been for a more deserving and innocent individual. He'd hired each and every one of these men based on a specific skillset, a measure of integrity beyond reproach, and sense of moral certainty in right and wrong.

Keane Sanderson, Royce Haverton, Brody Novak, Coen Flynn, and Sawyer Madison rounded out what was known as SSI—Safeguard Securities and Investigations. Townes owned and operated the agency, which provided contracted services to various law enforcement agencies when needed. The FBI and the U.S. Marshals Service were also included on that list, though this particular case was personal. It was a case he'd been involved with from the very beginning.

"Agent Gordon, would you please give me a moment alone with my team?"

Townes waited patiently for the FBI Senior Agent in Charge (SAIC) to comply with his request. It couldn't be easy for the man to have an outside agency pick apart his investigation and then find himself on the outside looking in. It most likely sucked as much as having to admit one's mistakes, but this wasn't a handholding moment to ease the ego of a veteran agent on the verge of retirement. He also shouldn't bear witness to what Townes was about to profess. Gordon would be bound by his oath to report his discovery to the courts.

"I guess I'll go and grab me another cup of crappy coffee then."

Agent Gordon didn't need to express his frustration. It was written all over his face as he grabbed his *Best Dad* ceramic mug off the pile of papers he had stacked in front of them on the conference table. The rest of his words were mumbled as the door closed behind him. Townes flipped a switch, which caused the glass walls to turn opaque and engage electronic counter-measures to defeat listening devices that weren't keyed to this type of jamming.

"I have a private plane waiting for you at Portland International Jetport," Brody stated, his clear image appearing on the large television attached to the far wall. His voice sounded somewhat digitized. The bright colors of his Hawaiian shirt were more than perceptible, but Townes hadn't employed him for his sense of style. The video feed to SSI's headquarters back in Florida was the only satellite location listening in on their conversation. This man had been able to make that happen without fear of exception. "The flight log will list Chicago O'Hare as your final destination. It will remain that way in writing. Your tail numbers and IFF squawk will change electronically to reflect that you are a C130 out of Great Lakes for the rest of the flight. No one will be able to determine your flight path other than the system once the tower clears you for takeoff. We have our own people at O'Hare to ensure that scenario happens without a hitch."

Townes didn't want to know the ins and outs of Brody's successes when it came to technology. He'd been hired for that reason, and he was excellent at his job.

"Good." Townes took his place at the head of the table. These men relied on him to give them the vital intelligence that could very well save their lives, and he'd been omitting a rather telling piece of information critical to any investigation. These specific details went to the perp's motives. "I want to cover some background about the time I spent with Ms. Doyle before Shepherd Moss entered the picture."

Townes took a moment to visually acknowledge every man sitting at the table in front of him. He respected each and every one, and it was obvious they returned the sentiment. Unfortunately, they would have every right to regard him differently after his forthcoming confession.

He stood by his actions, but he still braced himself for the recriminations from his team.

"We all served in the Corps. We know the toll that combat tours take on our bodies, as well as our inner selves. During those rather introspective times, I took my solace in motorcycles. I would mentally build one from the ground up and plan routes that I would take during my upcoming leave. I couldn't wait to enjoy the freedom of the open road."

Townes still owned the custom painted silver 2002 VRSC Harley Davidson he'd purchased the same day his boots hit United States' soil. That collection of metal had been his salvation—his steel and leather steed on which he could escape. It was still his desired method of getaway from the heavy weight of responsibilities he carried on his shoulders. He blamed this case and Shepherd Moss specifically for not having ridden for enjoyment in months. That needed to change soon.

"Anyway, I got involved with the one percenters due to an old friend having some issues he needed help in resolving. I came away from that time with loyal friendships, as well as underground connections that I have used when the need arose. These men don't play by the same rules, but there are times that rules need to be bent in order to see that justice is served."

Townes took a moment to share a look with Coen. His close combat specialist had very high morals when it came to right and wrong. It was one of the reasons he was on this team. Would that change once all the facts were on the table?

"A long story short, one of the members owed a rather prominent surgeon a favor for his assistance in not reporting a gunshot wound or two." Townes didn't have to explain who that doctor was by name, because recognition had dawned in each of their expressions. He would still tell his story so that no detail was left unstated. "Dr. Carter Doyle called in that favor by asking for personal protection for his only daughter who lived in the same area. You see, three of Shepherd Moss' victims had been found in the span of three months. All the women were from that same geographical area, though it was later when his predilections became known that the location had been nothing but a coincidence based on where Moss was residing at the time. Agent Gordon shared with the news outlets the only thing linking the victims from that region."

"They were all brunettes," Keane offered up, rubbing the back of his neck to ease the tension that no doubt had been there since SSI had taken this case. "And even that was a stretch, considering that Shailyn Doyle is actually a redhead. She'd darkened her hair back then. Age, race, profession, and anything else that usually tied victims together were missing. Why did Doyle have reason to believe his daughter was in danger? Now that I think about it, the only time that was addressed in the original case file was during the trial."

"That's right." Townes gestured toward the stack papers on the desk that were positioned in front of the now empty seat of Agent Gordon. The man had brought the pertinent case file should he need to reference it during the course of this briefing. "One of the victims had last been seen at a rather ritzy club that catered to the wealthier patrons in the area. Shailyn Doyle was part of that loose group of friends, and her father thought it best to have someone around for protection...especially on weekends. Someone who would blend in but could also create a barrier to someone approaching his daughter without a lot of embarrassing or uncomfortable questions having to be answered."

"How did you end up with that protection detail?" Coen's dark gaze was all but burning a hole in the front of Townes' dress shirt. The man was well aware that something was coming down the pike that would, without a doubt, affect the outcome of this manhunt they were currently involved with. "Were you personally involved with Shailyn Doyle at the time of her abduction?"

Townes allowed one corner of his lips to lift in admiration. No one had come right out and asked that direct question, though he understood that suspicion was shared widely among this team. He also didn't miss the fact Keane was studying the Armani suit jacket Townes was shrugging out of in his attempt at becoming somewhat more comfortable. That was a hard feat considering he was more at ease in a pair of faded jeans and a worn t-shirt.

He was a simple man at his core. Privacy was something he appreciated in all matters. He figured he had given enough of his mental, emotional, and physical wellbeing to serve the greater good that he could allow himself the luxury of enjoying a few of the finer things in life without scrutiny. He didn't overindulge in his outlaw lifestyle, not by any stretch of the imagination.

"I wasn't at the time I was asked to take the protective detail, but I was prior to her abduction." Townes trusted his response answered Coen's inquiry without giving too much information that would be disrespectful to Shailyn. Their connection had never been brought up in court as anything other than that of a business relationship. "Ms. Doyle was playing in Shepherd Moss' sandbox. Her father was right in assuming that she would most likely become a target sooner rather than later. Moss managed to get her out of the club that night without anyone the wiser. Unfortunately, that included me."

Townes didn't need to finish the rest of the story. Each and every one of them had read over the case file multiple times.

Shailyn Doyle had gone to the club one Friday night with a group of friends, unknowingly catching Moss' attention. She'd been a brunette back then, having dyed her hair to hide the beautiful shade of auburn she'd been born with. It was another fact that could have made all the difference had it been known publicly. It wasn't a surprise for Townes to see her during the first day of the trial with her natural color brought back to life. Unfortunately, the sparkle in her green eyes had long ago disappeared...along with her innocence.

"Moss held Ms. Doyle for three days before I tracked down his macabre workshop."

There was no other way to describe the abandoned warehouse where Moss had taken each of his victims, unless one referred to it as a death chamber. Townes had spent three days and two sleepless night combing through video footage of the club and each patron's movements. He sought out each man who'd entered the front doors of the establishment the night that Shailyn had been taken, discounting them one by one...until only one guilty individual remained.

The means and methods of Townes' search had never been recounted by law enforcement officials during the trial, nor by the men who'd suffered under his hands when he'd questioned them. His detailed description of what would happen to them should they talk had virtually guaranteed their silence. To this day, he never doubted their continued discretion.

"Calvert?"

Townes involuntarily made a fist at Sawyer's attempt to grab his attention, assuming Deputy U.S. Marshal Sturridge had arrived with his charge. A quick glance at the monitor revealed there were only two individuals standing on the other side of the now white windowpane, and neither one of them were the woman he sought.

How long had he been lost in thought?

"I was the one who located Moss' workshop, along with Shailyn Doyle who was just barely hanging on to life." Townes didn't bother to describe the scene. It was incomprehensible, the damage done to her body. Coen had caught a glimpse of Moss' handiwork a few days ago in Colorado. It was beyond vile, and what true evil represented in its most basic form. "You're aware from the case file that Moss was not at the scene at the time I arrived."

"Yes," Keane replied, lifting the folder that contained photographs of the crime scene. He'd been looking over the pictures for the hundredth time in hopes of something appearing that would lead them to Moss. "Traces of Ms. Doyle's blood was found in Moss' vehicle, as well as his bathroom sink and shower drains."

Coen abruptly pushed back his chair and leaned forward, rubbing his hands down his face in what was most likely frustration, if not outright denial. His unexpected movement grabbed everyone's attention. It wasn't long before the last piece of the puzzle fell into place. He steeled himself for the allegation that was yet to come.

"Son of a bitch," Brody murmured, his voice barely perceptible from the speaker.

Agent Gordon chose that moment to try and enter the conference room by knocking, but Townes held up a finger to pause his entrance. He could wait a moment longer. What Townes had to say was for his team only, and what they did with the information was up to them. He'd already paid the price for his sin ten times over by punishing himself.

"I won't verbally confirm what you already suspect, only due to our location." Townes wasn't about to confess to planting evidence in Moss' vehicle or place of residence in a federal office building. No one else had yet to comment. He wasn't sure they would, considering the fallout of what could come from something of that nature. "You should know that I had no doubt of that man's guilt and acted without fear of recrimination."

"We have your six, Calvert. No need to rehash this now." Royce looked over the table at Keane, who was nodding his agreement.

"According to the trial transcripts and subsequent juror interviews, it was Shailyn Doyle's testimony that put Shepherd Moss behind bars," Keane surmised, most likely already figuring out the reason for Townes' decision. It had taken over five days before the medical staff changed Shailyn's condition from critical to serious. All Townes had done was take out insurance, but not everyone would agree with that stance. "That's all I need to know."

"We're all good," Brody offered up, leaning closer to the camera.

Sawyer held up his Styrofoam coffee cup to signify that he was pleased with the way this meeting had gone. All eyes were now on Coen, who was the more serious of the group and took his responsibilities with the evidential chain of custody a little too far at times. He was the balance to Brody, who needed to be reined in more often than not. There was no better chemistry than this unit.

"What we saw in Colorado…" Coen's words drifted off as he shook his head to dispel the gruesome visions that still haunted them both. Townes had witnessed the vile destruction left behind by Moss twice, and that was two times too many. Evil like that could never be contained by simple walls and gates. He should have known better, and clearly Coen agreed. "You were far too kind, Calvert."

The gentlest of movement called Townes' attention to the monitor displaying the people waiting outside the conference room. He wasn't a man to be affected by a lot of things, but the beautiful vision before him was the exception.

Shailyn's green eyes met his through the video feed, and he couldn't stop his hand from flipping the switch and unlocking the now transparent windowpane. Their gazes connected until everything else faded away. She made it hard from him to breathe. The guilt he'd tried to ease through the years came back with a physical rush. It had been so long since he'd seen her that the smallest of changes were perceived by his discerning eye.

Her striking auburn tresses were longer, laying over her shoulders in waves as if she hadn't bothered to have her hair trimmed in months. The cream colored, long dress coat tied at the waist told him that she'd lost too much weight. Her porcelain skin hadn't seen the sun in what looked like months, though her cheeks had instantly flushed in reaction to setting eyes on him for the first since her trial. It didn't surprise him that the sparkle in those emerald green eyes of hers was still less than they had once held.

The need to see her smile return caught him off guard, but it was when she turned her back on him that the piercing culpability practically cut him in two. It had been his sole responsibility to protect her…and he'd failed.

"Sawyer, please collect Ms. Doyle." Townes shut down every single emotion running through his body as he reached for his suit jacket. He'd known where he stood with her long ago, so her response to his sudden presence shouldn't have been a surprise. "We have a lot of ground to cover before we head to Florida. It's best we get started immediately."

CHAPTER THREE

S HAILYN WAS TAKEN back in time the moment the windowpane became translucent. She immediately recognized those
gentle grey eyes.

Townes Calvert was breathtaking.

He would disagree with her. She understood that he wasn't
what most women would call handsome, but there was a strong
magnetism in his aura that was unmistakable.

She recalled distinctly the two-inch scar on his jawline and
the story behind it. She'd traced the black eagle, globe, and
anchor tattoo etched into his neck with her fingertips to the
point where she could draw the exact duplicate on paper. She
had...many times. She remembered the sensation of his long
brown hair caressing over her shoulders when he kissed her as if
it were just this morning. He still had the bump on the bridge of
his nose that she found endearing, much to his dismay. All of
that no longer mattered, though.

Shepherd Moss had most definitely seen to that.

"I'd like to go back to my house, please," Shailyn requested
softly, making sure her voice didn't carry through the opening
door of the conference room. She broke eye contact with the
one man who hurt her in a way Moss never could, and she
wasn't about to enter the ring for another round. "Now, please."

"Ms. Smith, you—"

"Please give up the pretense of calling me by that name." Shailyn was mentally tired of these security games. "You know very well what my name is, Deputy U.S. Marshal Sturridge. Now please take me back home or I'll be speaking to the U.S. Marshal for this district about your lack of cooperation."

"Ms. Smith, the gentleman you know as Townes Calvert is in fact a Special Chief Deputy U.S. Marshal appointed by the previous Director of the United States Marshals Service and the U.S. Attorney General. He is the ranking Chief Deputy U.S. Marshal in the region right now. It is not an honorary title. I have to follow his orders. I'm not even sure his team is aware of his connection to the service, among other things."

"Ms. Doyle?" Shailyn didn't bother to turn around at the sound of another man's voice. She would have felt slighted with Townes' inability to collect her himself had she not known where they stood with one another. "My name is Sawyer Madison. I work for SSI, Safeguard Securities and Investigations. I'm sure you're wondering—"

"No, I'm not wondering anything, Mr. Madison." Shailyn slipped her cold hands into the pockets of her dress coat. She balled her fingers into the palms of her hands. "Sturridge, I'll meet you downstairs. I'm not staying."

"I've heard a lot of amazing things about you, Shailyn. I'm surprised that you would want to leave without hearing us out first. You are key to our strategy."

Shailyn wouldn't allow herself to be played by someone with an obvious agenda. Sawyer Madison didn't know a thing about her other than what was in those files sitting on the conference table. Of that she was sure. Living through what Moss had done to her didn't make her amazing. It only made her physically weaker, mentally chaste, and very lucky. Or unlucky, depending on one's point of view.

She didn't miss a step as she walked around Sturridge. He was still as a statue.

Why would Townes come for her now?

That question nagged at Shailyn as she walked through the office door and down the long hallway to where the elevator banks were located. The black suit he'd been wearing made him seem to be a part of either the FBI or the U.S. Marshals Service. It was hard to believe that he would have joined the federal government in any enterprise, especially considering his affiliation to the one percent motorcycle clubs. She wondered if he was still a patched member bearing the Nomad rocker.

Why was she even curious?

What Townes did with his life was of no concern to her.

"Shailyn."

His voice brought her up short, as if a wall had appeared. There was a raspiness to his tone that was discernable only to him. She closed her eyes to ward off the onrushing memories, knowing she could never go back and reclaim her past from the wreckage.

"There's nothing to say, Gunny," Shailyn whispered, having no doubt that he heard her use his charter name.

It wasn't coincidental that the nickname for his rank in the Corps and his charter name were the same. He'd gone by that handle for so long that at one point a large number of his associates in the one percent world never knew his given name. She'd had the privilege to know that particular nuance due to the closeness of their relationship at the time.

She was afraid to speak in a normal tone for fear she'd break down, but she didn't want to appear weak. She cleared her throat and gathered what courage she had left. It was easier to use his familiar nickname as a form of self-defense, letting him know that she was a part of the past he'd left behind. He was a remembrance she would have given anything to have back, but that would never happen.

"You shouldn't have come here. You're not welcome."

Shailyn forced her legs to move forward once again. It was getting harder and harder to breathe the longer she remained in his presence. He had taken all the air out of the building.

"Moss didn't give either of us a choice."

And there it was. He'd been forced to this conclusion. Townes hadn't come to Maine for her. He'd come because of Moss. His intention wasn't to help the U.S. Marshals transfer her to another small town under a different banal name in order to maintain her anonymity. He wanted Shepherd Moss, and the only way to draw him out was through her as bait.

"You always have a choice, Gunny. Moss isn't in charge of your agenda. Or is he?" Shailyn braced herself as she turned around to face him. Her attempt at composure almost cracked before she managed to slip it in place. His grey eyes saw too much. She wondered if he could still read her like a book. She fought the urge to tug her black turtleneck a little higher to hide the scars. "It doesn't matter. *I* still have a choice. And I'm choosing to go back to the life that was created for me. You don't need me to solve your problems."

"Moss *will* eventually find you." Townes turned the tables a bit, causing her to question his original intention. "It's only a matter of time."

Shailyn came very close to asking why he thought she would be better off with him, but she stopped herself before the words could escape. He would take her sentiment the wrong way. It was abundantly clear that he still blamed himself for what had happened to her all those years ago. He couldn't see past his precious, self-involved guilt to recognize the truth—only one man was responsible for what was done to her. His name was Shepherd Moss.

"Moss has had over four months to find me," Shailyn pointed out, refusing to be drawn into a debate that neither one of them would win. "Other than you placing me at risk by bringing me here tonight, what makes today any different from yesterday?"

A strand of his long brown hair came loose from the tie at the base of his neck, but it didn't hide the fact that his scar turned white in response to his clenched jaw. He seemed to think she was purposefully making his job harder than it needed to be in terms of her consent.

"What is it exactly you want from me, Townes?"

"I want you to come back home to Florida with me."

Shailyn had to literally force herself to relax her hands. Her nails had dug into her palms at the mention of where her parents still resided. She hadn't seen her mother and father for many years, though she had been officially reprimanded when the U.S. Marshals had discovered she'd contacted her parents by phone a couple of weeks ago. It was as if they'd expected her to shut off any emotions she had in her previous life due to their desire for seamless security.

Now, Townes wanted to take her home. Ignoring the double entendre, she wondered if he thought he could give her a taste of what she craved, only to then steal it away again? She wasn't capable of handling the impact of that anymore.

"No. I can't."

Shailyn hadn't expected Townes to close the distance between them, but he slowly advanced until he stood mere inches from her. She tried not to breathe, but it became involuntary. The faint scent of his cologne took away the years as if they were nothing more than dandelions gone to seed, blowing away in the wind. She was already shaking her head to deny his attempt to change her mind.

"I am so sorry."

Those four words were said with such tender sincerity that he brought an immediate cascade of tears to her eyes. The remorse written across his rugged features broke her heart all over again. She tentatively reached up and found herself stroking his scar with her thumb in comfort.

"Had you come to me back then during the trial, I would have told you that you had nothing to be sorry for," Shailyn murmured, hoping her words eased whatever guilt he still held close to his heart. All she'd ever wanted back then was for him to hold her and tell her it would all be okay. Instead, he'd turned into himself and believed he was solely to blame for her maiming. He was also mistaking her refusal to help him now due to a retaliation of sorts. That couldn't be further from the truth. "It was my own mistake that put me in Moss' path, not yours nor anyone else's."

"I was hired to protect you," Townes reminded her forceful-ly, though he didn't pull away from her touch. His grey eyes darkened upon his confession. "Instead, I became involved with you. I lost sight of my objective. I failed."

"That isn't the truth, and it certainly isn't the reason I'm walking away now."

Shailyn noticed right away that his warmth had radiated into her hand. She hadn't felt heat like that in a very long time, so it was very hard for her to pull away. She did so anyway and let her hand drop as she took a step back.

"Why are you walking away when I'm offering you the chance to come out of hiding?"

"You aren't offering me a chance at salvation, Townes." Shailyn wished more than anything it didn't have to be this way.

"There is nothing I can do to prevent Moss from going after the people I love. Hasn't he already proven that to you? Moss is on the Top Ten Most Wanted list, which means that the federal government will continue to monitor my family and close friends. Coming out of WITSEC could very well end that courtesy."

"I won't let that happen. I have the authority to continue their protection details until we resolve this case. My credentials don't just consist of those with the U.S. Marshals Service."

Shailyn didn't doubt that Townes had done well for himself over the years. He wasn't the same man she knew so long ago when he'd been so full of anger, bound for infamy. It was more than apparent he'd conquered at least some of the demons he had left over from the war, but he seemed to have replaced them with other more frightening lords. That was something she hadn't asked for, and she would gladly take them back if it meant he could be free from the evil that had occupied her life thus far.

"Moss isn't targeting only those close to you, Shailyn, and you know it," Townes replied harshly, reminding her of those recent deaths that lay solely at her feet. Did he think she was so callous as not to feel remorse? "He's been trying to draw you out since the day he escaped federal prison. Let's give him what he wants, because it will only be then that he makes his mistake. Subsequently, and once and for all, I can correct my mistake."

Shailyn so wanted to take Townes up on his offer, but una-dulterated fear could be very crippling if one took heavy doses of it on a daily basis for three years. There were moments in her life where she'd thought that nothing could ever bring back the terror she'd once experienced, but then there were times like these that made her stand corrected.

"And what if he doesn't make a mistake?" Shailyn managed to say through her dry lips as each and every scar on her body throbbed in memory. "What if Moss succeeds this time, and I have to endure every cut he sliced into my skin once again? What then, Townes? Will you end my suffering?"

ANOTHER DAY HAD passed without progress. These were the hours that were the hardest, but he would persevere as he always had.

Was Shailyn thinking of him? Was she in fear?

He gradually smiled as he blew out the candle, that lone breath descending him into complete darkness.

CHAPTER FOUR

NOTHING TOWNES SAID could convince Shailyn to believe he could protect her, because the truth of the matter was that he couldn't get inside Moss' mind. Oh, he could definitely try to figure out the likely avenues of approach, but nothing was ever a hundred percent guaranteed...as their shared past had certainly shown them.

"You know firsthand I can't promise you anything, but I now know who we're dealing with." Every law enforcement agency had traditionally underestimated their opponent back when Moss had first come onto their radar. No one had ever considered from the start that they'd be dealing with such a highly intelligent psychopath. He was a cunning animal who had the unique ability to blend in with the shadows and virtually disappear in plain sight. "I've taken precautions that I've designed to benefit us while serving as a constant detriment to Moss. This is our chance, Shailyn. I'm afraid if we don't take the initiative at this late stage, there won't be another opportunity to force Moss to react to our decisions instead of his."

Townes had purposefully acquired open landscaped property in Florida with every intention of creating her a fortress that was nearly impenetrable to a clandestine attack by a small party or even a single assailant. The security system in place was similar to those of some large corporate retreats like the National Conference Center in Leesburg, Virginia or the President's retreat at Camp David. He wasn't being generous in that comparison, either.

He'd also hired a technological specialist who was proficient with specialized anti-intrusion sensors and integrated security hardware. The brilliant man could maintain and service the software needed to sustain the network of multilayered equipment endlessly scanning the grounds and skies for anything moving in the vicinity of the compound.

The connections Townes had cultivated over the years had been made with one goal in mind, and that was to guarantee Shailyn Doyle's future if they needed to fall back to the Alamo. He'd done a lot of things in his life that he regretted, but none more so than allowing her to suffer unspoken amounts of pain at the hands of a monstrous genius devoid of empathy. It was only fair that she know his end game, but not right now and definitely not here.

"And what is this chance you speak of, Townes?" Shailyn glanced past him in apprehension to where his team was still gathered in the small field office. "Do you really think that Moss is foolish enough to try and simply abduct me in broad daylight with several law enforcement agencies watching my every move? Have you designed a new mousetrap?"

"No." Townes purposefully turned sideways, allowing her an unobstructed view of the path he needed her to take. "But if you'll give me and my team a chance to explain, you'll see that we have the ability to end this."

Townes hadn't realized his muscles had been so taut until she took a tentative step forward. He honestly wasn't sure what he would have done had she turned and walked toward the elevator at the end of the hall. The need to end this hell she'd been living in was what had gotten him out of bed each morning. She'd been his sole focus for years, and that wasn't about to change anytime soon. He was now committed to this course of action.

Shailyn finally came to a stop in front of him, tilting her head back and studying him with those emerald green eyes of hers. She had a dusting of freckles over the bridge of her nose that he'd found so attractive when they'd first met. The flush on her cheeks earlier had faded though, leaving only the pale truth behind.

When had she last slept a full night?

He resisted the urge to ask her anything personal. Now wasn't the time, and he wasn't sure *he* was ready for those specific answers.

"You keep saying *we*." Shailyn gently licked her lips before inquiring about recent events Sturridge had shared with her. "Has this hunt become personal again?"

Townes didn't bother to reply that this manhunt had always been personal. That much should have been obvious to her. He wouldn't withhold information from her, though. He involuntarily rested his hand gently on her lower back as he guided her down the hall.

"Moss also targeted the sister of one of my team members." Townes thought back to when Camryn Novak had bruises around her neck. She was also involved with Sawyer, which Moss had used to his advantage. She'd barely made it out of that hotel room alive as a result of several stupid mistakes and just a bit of luck. So yes, it wasn't a stretch to assume that the members of SSI had taken that as a direct threat to hearth and home. "He's coming at this puzzle from every angle until he hits pay dirt."

"You mean until he finds and kills me."

Townes shifted his body so that he was between Shailyn and the door. It was selfish of him really, but he needed to be able to truly see her without being judged by the men in the other room. He needed to confirm for himself that he'd done the right thing by staying far away from her throughout the years.

"Don't box me in," Shailyn warned softly as she stared at the firearm in his holster before stepping back. It was the first time she refused to meet his gaze. "There's no need to rehash the decisions we made in the past."

"You mentioned something that needs to be ironed out before we continue this, because I don't want there to be any misunderstandings between us."

Townes was well aware of how he looked to others outside of the military and this world he'd created for himself. He didn't fit into the stereotypical mold of a corporate security company owner and operator. Honestly, he liked it that way. As an executive appointee to Special Chief Deputy U.S. Marshal, he had a wide reach with few limitations. But nothing excused what he now understood to be the proverbial monkey wrench in the works. It was something they would both need to deal with in their own way, but that would have to be at a later date and time.

"It wasn't my choice to deny your request to see me, Shailyn." Townes didn't want to have this conversation here, but this subject needed to be touched on so that she understood he wasn't doing this out of some sense of guilt. It was so much more. "I honored your father's wishes not to see you after the night I brought you to the hospital, but he was right. It was better that way. I would have exposed you to more damage."

Townes pulled open the heavy door before she could reply, because there was nothing she could say that would change the past or his decision. Carter Doyle had done what he thought best for his daughter, and he'd been right in doing so. She most likely would have refused to go into WITSEC, or Townes might very well have offered to go into the program with her. Neither would have worked out very well at the time.

He sure as hell wouldn't be in the position he was in now to eliminate Shepherd Moss as a threat.

As it was, Moss *would* be back in custody shortly…or dead.

The latter was preferable, but Townes had men waiting for him in the conference room to consider before breaking any laws that would affect their futures as well as his.

"It seems we have a lot to talk about then," Shailyn murmured, not having a choice but to follow his lead since all eyes were tracking their progress across the open-spaced office. He was surprised when she caught hold of his hand. "I need to understand just one thing first."

Townes didn't want to do this here, so he took another step forward in hopes to guide her along without further delay. She apparently had other plans.

"Would you have stood next to me during that trial had my father not asked you to stay away?"

Townes should have given her any answer but the truth. Their past didn't matter to anyone but them. They were fighting for her future, which didn't consist of just another name in another town, with another life.

"Yes."

He gently removed his hand and waited for her to precede him into the conference room. Sawyer stood and indicated that Shailyn should take a seat toward the front of the room where Townes would be addressing the team, as well as Agent Gordon and Deputy U.S. Marshal Sturridge.

"Let's get the introductions out the way, shall we?" Townes was now in his element of strictly business. Any reservations he had that this was the right decision faded away now that Shailyn was surrounded by the most qualified and dangerous men in the business. He pushed aside all emotion as he got down to the task at hand. "I'm sure you remember Agent Gordon."

Shailyn tentatively smiled in acknowledgement, her inquisitive gaze landing on the other men. Time was of the essence, so names would have to do for now.

"To your left is Sawyer Madison, Keane Sanderson, and Royce Haverton. Across from you is Coen Flynn, and on the screen in front of us is Brody Novak. These men round out SSI and will be your personal protection detail from this point forward until Moss is captured. Each man is a highly trained, dedicated professional."

"And what is your plan to capture Moss?" Shailyn asked, turning the chair with her knee-high black boot. She hadn't bothered to remove her long wool coat, which was for the best, considering they would be leaving this building in under five minutes. "Are you leaking my whereabouts to the press or just the junkie grapevine?"

"No." Townes leaned forward and pressed his palms onto the hardwood surface of the table in determination. What he was about to propose wasn't up for debate. The details had been carefully laid out and it was now time to pull the trigger. "As of ten minutes ago, your death was reported on national television. Shailyn Doyle is dead."

CHAPTER FIVE

S HAILYN STARED OUT the small oval window of the
Gulfstream G650, hardly noticing the sunrise. A couple of
the men had asked if she was okay when they noticed she wasn't
sleeping. There was no reason to worry them with the truth, so
she lied and said she was fine. It made them feel better and took
the pressure off her to explain.

"Here." A porcelain coffee cup was presented to her instead
of the usual Styrofoam ones given to the passengers on
airplanes. The man with the blond hair and boyish face took the
seat across from her, though his cute dimple wasn't showing at
the moment. "I thought you could use some caffeine if you're
not going to sleep."

They were less than an hour away from landing in Sanford,
Florida, but it wouldn't have mattered the location.

She was dead to the world.

"You're angry with Calvert for making that unilateral decision." Sawyer Madison settled back into his seat as if they were
discussing the weather. "I understand why you're upset. Even
your parents don't know the truth, but their reaction at your
funeral needs to be very real."

Shailyn remained silent as she looked down at the coffee in
her hands. He'd given it to her black, just the way she preferred.

It should have been disconcerting that he had knowledge of such a private thing, but nothing bothered her now that her life was not her own any longer.

"You're mistaken." She took a tentative sip of the steaming java, surprised at the rich smoothness. This wasn't standard rent-a-jet coffee. "I'm not angry. Aside from that one phone call to my father that I know you're very well aware of, I haven't spoken to my parents since I entered WITSEC. The definition of death can be taken so many different ways."

Shailyn couldn't help but seek out Townes, who had been on the other side of the plane going over various files. He never left her side until she was seated on the plane, and even then stayed close enough to keep his eyes on her at a glance.

She was still coming to terms with the fact that her father had been the one responsible for keeping her and Townes apart during the whole trial process. All this time she'd thought it was either his guilt or the fact that her body was covered in more scars than he would ever acquire in two lifetimes. The two technically went hand in hand. Either way, her father had no right to make decisions on her behalf. She was her own woman and always had been. He also didn't deserve to think that his only daughter was dead without an explanation.

"What exactly does Townes hope to accomplish by faking my death?" Shailyn hadn't given up her long winter coat, although she had taken her arms out of the sleeves. The lapels laid over her shoulders for extra warmth. It wasn't nearly enough. "Wouldn't that mean Moss is free to move on to other women?"

"Yes and no." Sawyer shot her a grin, allowing that dimple of his to form. His blue eyes sparkled with optimism, yet there was a solemnity one couldn't miss. "Moss is too intelligent to take the press release at face value. He'll need to confirm it. He's going to want to believe you died from complications of what transpired under his hand, but he won't be able to let you go without looking into it."

"Which means Moss has to come out of hiding to get to the root cause of my death," Shailyn surmised, still not comprehending why Townes and his men thought this strategy could work. "We all know that he won't do that. He'll have one of his minions do his dirty work."

"Which is why no one can know the truth." Sawyer shifted his legs so that they were stretched out into the aisle. It appeared he was mulling over his strategy before he continued speaking. "It will make it harder for Moss to confirm your death. He'll want your autopsy report, thereby giving us the time to investigate a developing lead we think could steer us straight to him."

"And what *promising* lead would that be?"

Townes chose that moment to look up from the file in his hand. His grey eyes immediately met hers. He'd unbuttoned his sleeves and rolled them up to his elbows, as well as loosened the blue and black tie around his neck. No amount of expensive apparel could hide what he truly was—a strange blend of an old-fashioned warrior.

He was half Chiricahua Apache, or *Aiaha* as they called themselves on his father's side, along with a mixed bag of Scottish Highlander and everything else on his mother's side. It made for a very stoic breed of fighter that never quit. Once he latched onto something, he would hunt it down to the bitter end, forsaking all other comforts until he could face his enemy in personal combat.

What would he say if she were to tell him that *he* was the reason she struggled to survive?

"There was a fifth-grade teacher who went missing decades ago," Sawyer explained, folding his hands over his middle as he settled in to tell her the story. "Her body was found around five years ago in a forest by some naturalist out for a hike, but no one was ever charged for her murder, because there was so little evidence left by the time they found the body. You see, Caroline Marinovic taught in the same small school district where Shepherd Moss was a student. He was twelve years old when…"

A low buzzing began in her mind, almost as if to camouflage Sawyer's words once the name *Caroline* triggered an uneasiness that she hadn't experienced in a very long time. Flashes of the past began to form and shift before her eyes but just as quickly faded. She focused on Sawyer so he wouldn't recognize her outward signs of an anxiety attack.

"…and her fiancé still teaches at the same high school. We need Moss' attention diverted while we investigate close to his childhood home. We need his focus on our distraction while we dig up the bones of his past."

"Because you think that's where he's hiding right now, don't you?" Shailyn tightened her grip on the mug to stop her fingers from trembling. She needed to gather her composure before stepping one foot outside of this plane. She should be a pro at relocating by now, but she'd always done so alone. "Do you think this woman's fiancé is helping Moss? Why would he do that? Have you contacted him?"

"We're not sure of anything right now, but it's a promising thread we need to unravel. Caroline Marinovic had similar markings on her bones that would indicate…"

The low hypnotic humming once again tried to draw her into the past, and this time the enticement was too much to resist. Lights flashed until her vision tunneled and lured her right back to the gates of hell.

"…*does it feel? Are you past the pain, Caroline? Or have you come to yearn for it?*"

The agonizing penetration of the blade in her side had her screaming out as he slowly took his time to work the knife into her flesh. A part of her hoped this would be the last one, but something told her this was just the beginning of the next level.

"Shailyn." The warmth of Townes' hands on hers jolted her back to the present before she cleared her vision to see that he was kneeling before her in the aisle. He appeared by her side as if by teleportation. He was such a large man that she still had to look up to meet his worried gaze. "Are you okay?"

Townes had taken the coffee she'd been holding and handed it off to Sawyer. He was asking her something, but she couldn't get her thoughts in order to interpret what his words meant. She parted her lips to tell him what she'd remembered.

Caroline.

Shailyn couldn't make her voice work. The fear had robbed her of speech. The panic at being taken to a place she only ever involuntarily visited in her nightmares was washing over her in waves. It was as overwhelming as the tides. One specific cut below the bottom of her left rib throbbed in remembrance of the blade being pulled out so gradually that the sickening sound of suction along the blood le or blood groove released her body's grasp on the instrument could still be heard.

She understood this to be folly. The nonsense about a long flat channel on a blade for blood to flow along to reduce suction was an old soldier's tale. Physics didn't work that way, but she recalled the suction as the length of the knife was withdrawn. She cleared her throat and tried to speak again.

"Caroline." Shailyn finally managed to say the name, immediately initiating a tremor of disgust that traveled through her entire body. "He called me Caroline during our time together."

"Sawyer, get ahold of Brody and tell him our timetable just moved up," Townes instructed in a tone that broke no argument. Sawyer instantly vacated the seat and had his phone to his ear before he took one step down the aisle. "Shailyn, are you sure that—"

"Don't," Shailyn warned as she yanked her hands from his. Whatever warmth he'd managed to give her instantaneously evaporated into space. "Do not treat me like a child who isn't sure where she put her favorite doll."

"I'm sorry." Townes pressed upward and unwound back into the seat rather abruptly, obviously going for a different approach. She didn't appreciate being handled as if she were made of some fragile piece of glass. Everyone always assumed that she was weak because of what she'd gone through. She had been forged in the fire—not broken. They all would mention how strong she must have been to survive such a horrible ordeal, but then they spoke to her as if she were a delicate china teacup. It was insulting. Coming from someone as close as Townes made it even worse. "It wasn't my intention to—"

"I was chained down to a table for three days, Townes." Shailyn inhaled a breath, albeit shakily. Her coat had fallen lower in her seat when she had leaned forward, so she took her time drawing it upward and back over her shoulders. He didn't say a word as she settled back and tucked her hair behind her ears before she went into more detail. "I can recall almost every minute of the first day, but I'd lost consciousness several times by the second. I would fade in and out, usually when Moss wanted to talk to me as he worked. There are times when bits and pieces come back to me unexpectedly, as if playing on my very own motion picture screen."

"You mean when something or someone triggers a flash-back. Do you remember the trigger?"

Shailyn remembered that the scar on his jawline would whit-en when something bothered or irritated him, but only now did she notice the way his lips thinned out when referring to her past. He wasn't the only one who had a ticket to play the blame game. She was the one who'd purposefully slipped off to the restroom by herself without his knowledge because she'd been angry with him about something stupid.

"He called me Caroline." Shailyn was used to the nausea that rolled over her upon thinking back on that time, and now was no different. She rested a hand against her abdomen to keep it at bay and intentionally evened out her breathing until the queasiness had dissipated. "How does this change the direction of the investigation?"

"It doesn't." Townes surprised her by leaning forward and reaching for the straps of the seatbelt on either side of her. In her opinion, securing her into the seat was a rather intimate gesture. She didn't miss that he only ever rested his hand on her lower back…nowhere else. The metal pieces snapped together with a solid click, but Townes didn't immediately pull away. "What can I do, Shailyn?"

The quiet inquiry didn't need an explanation. He was asking what he could do for her to help her through the upcoming days, weeks, and possibly months of baiting a killer to come out to play. It was a very sweet gesture, but her reply had him pulling away as if she'd slapped him.

"You can stop being so hesitant around me, Townes." Shailyn gave him a small smile to take the sting out of her words. "I'm still the woman you were once so close to. I'm still the same woman you took to bed just hours before we walked into that club."

RAGE.

That was the sole emotion running through his body at watching the headline news.

Did Townes Calvert really believe that he would fall for such a completely amateur stunt?

Shailyn Doyle was not dead.

She was alive and well.

He would know if it was true. He would feel it throughout his entire being.

The pretty blonde news anchor continued to explain the falsified details of a death that was nothing more than a ploy. Did the collective federal agencies believe he was that gullible?

No. They understood exactly who they were dealing with, which is why a seed of doubt had been planted. Was there truth to what was being reported?

He quietly walked into the small kitchenette as the low murmur of the television faded away. A blanket of serenity slowly washed over him as his fury diminished. He opened the cupboard and withdrew a glass before filling it to exactly one-half inch below the rim with water from the tap. The mundane task allowed his rather muddled thoughts to finally clear with its precision.

Shailyn's death would need to be confirmed, of course. It was a relatively easy thing to do that he could delegate without getting his hands dirty.

He didn't even bother to contemplate the choice he would have to make if such a revelation was true. After all, that would only be a waste of his precious time.

CHAPTER SIX

TOWNES TOOK HIS time making his version of a steaming cup of black coffee from his personal DeLonghi machine. He combined two shots of expresso with a splash of RO water to the ground Jamaican Blue Mountain beans to the precise desired consistency. The grinds were about the same size as refined white sugar.

He packed the double-shot maker with a practiced hand. The resulting flavor was beyond anything one could find in any world-renowned five-star restaurant. The best part of the process was creating such a delicacy in the privacy of his own office.

It wasn't that he didn't drink the coffee from the kitchen every now and then when he was running short on time. Unfortunately, the grinds were coarser for the drip machine and didn't produce the same flavor he preferred. That type of coffee was strong enough for most natives, but too weak for his tastes.

He carried his idea of perfection, along with the case file he'd been reading over, to his comfortable leather chair in the far corner of his office facing the closed door on the inside wall. The outer walls of the estate buildings were made of heavy thick natural logs that could easily stop a .30 caliber bullet. Even the windows were to be covered in the event of an attack with interlocking steel shutters that rolled down in seconds from encasements anchored to the eaves above.

He'd created all of this for one woman.

Townes carefully set down the mug on the heavy ceramic tray he'd acquired from an antique store. In fact, it was the same small boutique that he'd gotten the early American side table from in his hunt for the right furniture. He then tossed the manila folder on the oak desk in front of him.

The appraiser had tracked the lineage of the 1700s English-style desk to Revolutionary War-era New Jersey. A man outside of Trenton who went by the name of Everton claimed to be quite the Tory, but he was in fact an agent of Washington's who had tracked English troop movements during the war. The idea of Everton's letters being written on this very desk helping Washington to time his own movements had tweaked Townes' sense of intrigue.

He'd purposefully chosen a traditional early American motif for this room as an escape. The rich, earth-tone colors of the wood offered a simple relaxing quality that at times he desperately needed.

This was one of those moments.

He needed to decompress.

Shailyn remained as beautiful as he remembered, if not more so. Those emerald green pools of emotion managed to hide the pain and suffering she'd endured during her time with Moss, but nearly failed in the efforts to conceal her constant apprehension. She handily converted her anxiety into contempt, mostly funneled toward him. It was simmering just underneath the surface waiting to vent in some spectacular fashion. He suspected that his scars would multiply during their forthcoming engagements…at least, the psychological ones.

Townes tried to maintain his distance, giving her the time

and space she required to digest the proposed plan. It wouldn't be easy for her to allow her parents and other family members to believe she was dead, but there was no other choice to be had.

He convinced himself it was entirely for their own safety, which wasn't far from the truth considering Moss' penchant for attacking from oblique angles. The twisted killer needed to trust that the woman he desperately wanted to have back for his own amusements was no longer alive. He was torn by the need to finish his work. Only then could he move on and eventually make the mistake that would land him back into federal custody. Townes was certain Moss was in search of the quintessential moment where he recognized his path forward. That trail led directly to Shailyn.

As it stood, the next couple of hours would be spent re-searching the people involved with Caroline Marinovic's investigation—the moment Moss began his dark journey. It would kill the time needed for Brody to set things in motion for their road trip south to the scene of Marinovic's demise. The more the pieces of the puzzle settled into place, the closer they came to Moss' current location.

Townes had devoted the majority of the morning seeing to it that Shailyn was settled into a guest room on the upper level of his home. He'd ordered that the compound be prepositioned at a higher level of readiness. The shutters on all the windows had been lowered, locked into place, and raised again by a few inches for gaps to allow light to shine through between the slats.

The weight of the security shutters would take only a second to close to a solid protective wall should the need arise. The system would automatically do so every evening at sundown.

Pickets were established between buildings. Townes had hired additional security personnel to pad the rolls of those available to walk post. No electronic device could ever replace a sentry in Townes' mind. Anything electronic could be spoofed. Brody had made that abundantly clear.

Shailyn was adapting to her new environment. She didn't have a lot of luggage, and he was honestly surprised when she'd mentioned that the two bags were everything she owned. Brody had gone over her laptop and electronic devices to ensure there wasn't any possibility of a breach while providing her access to their network.

Townes didn't like that Shailyn had taken to being such a minimalist. Having a new life in WITSEC meant she should have been able to start over with a new identity and existence. People tended to collect items that were needed in their daily lives. She had little to show for the life she'd led since her testimony and inception into the nether world of witness protection.

Remnants of anger stirred inside of him. Shailyn hadn't taken advantage of what the witness protection program had to offer.

She hadn't started anew.

He'd imagined her teaching at some community college, shopping with friends, and enjoying the anonymity and freedom Moss had taken from her as Shailyn Doyle. Instead, she'd chosen to hide herself away from everything and everyone, forsaking life in favor of her own personal refuge away from society.

Had he made a mistake in allowing the U.S. Marshals Service leeway in creating Shailyn a new identity? Should he have personally gotten involved and attended to the details himself? It would have allowed him the ability to make sure that she didn't retreat into a hole where she would suffer alone. He could have easily pulled some favors in creating her a new life, maybe even over in England or France.

"Got a minute?"

Townes wasn't surprised to find Coen at the entrance of his

office. He'd purposefully left the door open in case Shailyn needed anything, but to also signify that he was available for conversations with his team. He'd delivered a rather stunning blow earlier, and there was no doubt they would want to discuss his breach of proper justice in more detail.

"Yes." Townes took a seat in the plush leather seat on wheels, indicating Coen should do the same in one of the two guest chairs in front of his desk. "Have Sawyer and Royce been in touch with Brody yet?"

"No, but it's still early." Coen held a glass of orange juice in his hand, preferring the acidic drink over the smooth richness of the coffee Townes had imported from Jamaica. Coen had shaved since his assignment up in Colorado, but a five o'clock shadow had formed after their last forty-eight hours in Maine. "I want to do an aerial sweep of the county where Catherine Marinovic's body was found. I can get a head start if I leave for the airport now."

Townes pushed back his chair when he realized that Coen hadn't stopped by to discuss the past sins he'd admitted to earlier. No one seemed to deem his actions relevant to the present case, yet he'd made the disclosure out of necessity in his own mind. He found it odd that they weren't wondering just how far he would go in the end to see to it that Shailyn had some semblance of a life after this was all said and done. Or did they accept that he would do what was needed? Hell, maybe they would do the same.

"The aerial sweep has already been done. Brody has the full report and video files." Townes opened the folder that was resting on the ottoman and pulled out the high-resolution images that displayed several distinctive areas where remote cabins were located off the grid. He'd already circled numerous properties that could potentially harbor Moss without ever catching someone's interest. "You and Keane will be given the coordinates of the higher priority target locations. Take Brody's Wrangler as far inland as possible before then venturing off on foot. Make sure the two of you pack the essential items needed—an emergency beacon and two satellite phones with additional battery packs. The M4s are all cleaned and ready to go. Each has a pouch with six thirty-round magazines and a speed loader. Throw in a couple extra ammo cans of M855."

"Do I want to know when you had time to order up all this coverage?" Coen asked as he stepped forward and took the proffered photographs. He studied the different areas Townes had already designated on the overlay map before lifting one corner of his mouth in a sardonic smile. "You know, sleep does come in handy now and then for us human beings. The experts actually say it's healthy for you."

"Someone else had some wise words about sleeping when one was dead."

Townes took a seat in his favorite chair and repressed a moan of comfort. He'd taken a shower earlier, shedding the tailored Armani suit and silk necktie that he would have liked to throw in the trash. As far as he was concerned, ties were an altogether bad idea with the exception of making wonderful tourniquets when needed. Unfortunately, there were times he needed to dress the part of a business owner to blend in with the movers and shakers he needed to back his efforts up on the Hill.

Today had been one of those days, though he was now wearing his most comfortable pair of jeans and a plain black Harley t-shirt. He'd collected many over the thousands of hours spent on the back of his bike.

"No offense, but that person probably is dead and gone." Coen studied the satellite images in silence, making no move to leave the office. It appeared he had more to say. "Danny received a year for violating his parole. He'll most likely be out in six to eight months for good behavior."

Townes didn't bother to let Coen know he'd already been apprised of Danny Flynn's court appearance. It couldn't be easy for a man like Coen to have a brother on the other side of the law. He didn't need to know that Townes had already arranged for Danny's commissary account.

"Is there anything you need?"

"The crimes that Danny committed can't be compared to the small transgression you made to ensure Moss was put behind bars."

Townes knew that not to be true. He'd broken the law just the same. It didn't matter that it had prevented several women's deaths or that the end justified the means. This was Coen's way of saying that he would let bygones be bygones. It was also his way of indicating that he understood the reasoning behind Townes' decision.

"Thanks."

There was nothing more Townes could say in response so he left it at that. This topic was now closed, and they could all move forward.

"I'll go tell Keane that we're—"

Townes' cell phone rang, cutting off Coen in midsentence. A look at the display read *unknown caller*.

"Calvert."

"Do you miss her?" For just a moment, Townes thought he'd heard wrong. He had to be mistaken. "I do."

"Moss. I have to admit this is quite a surprise."

Coen's look of disbelief didn't stop him from quickly walking to Townes' desk. He grabbed the receiver off the landline base, holding the phone against his shoulder as he stabbed one of the buttons. He managed to set down the glass of orange juice before quietly alerting Brody to what was transpiring. With any luck, he'd be able to trace this call to at least an area code and hopefully bring this entire manhunt to a close.

"Is it? Really?" Moss paused as if considering what to say next. Maybe he was watching a clock and gauging how much time he had before his location was revealed. "I had momentarily entertained the thought that perhaps Shailyn's death might be nothing but a ploy of yours."

This was the sole reason Townes needed Shailyn's death to be as authentic as possible. Moss was far too intelligent to fall for a simple statement read on a teleprompter by a news anchor.

"That would have to be quite an elaborate setup, wouldn't it?" Townes asked, wondering just how far Moss would take this conversation.

"An attending physician at the hospital was very forthcoming in describing in detail Shailyn's breathing complications toward the end." Moss had taken the bait and located the physician SSI had purposefully paid to play a role in this deception. Something of this nature wasn't done haphazardly. Townes had started the ball rolling within a month of Moss' break from federal prison. "It's amazing what people will say or do for money. I'm sure the monetary donation to his bank account will help this holiday season."

Townes wasn't sure which focus Moss meant for that declaration to be directed. Was he implying that the doctor was paid off by SSI, or did he simply mean he offered money for the information he'd received?

A quick glance at Coen let him know they needed this conversation to continue for a successful trace. He was moving his hand in a continuous circle while listening intently for Brody's announcement of triumph.

"It appears you were successful in the end," Townes credited before steering this discussion in another direction. "Are you going to hide in your hole until I find you? I suggest you make this easy on yourself, Moss. Turn yourself in this afternoon and stop wasting both of our time."

"And here I thought this would have you moving on to bigger and better opportunities."

"You thought wrong. I'm going to take you off the street." Townes rarely allowed himself to experience the built-up rage that was buried deep inside his soul, but he needed Moss to fully believe this ruse they'd erected to deceive him. His part had finally arrived. "Understand this, you demented fuckstick. I will not stop hunting you until you are either back in chains or preferably six feet under the ground in a potter's field. You will pay for what you put Shailyn Doyle through, as well as those other eighteen women. Or should I say nineteen? I know all about Caroline Marinovic. I know how you see her face in every one of your victims, but I can guarantee you that it will be my face that you see as you take your last breath. That's a promise."

Townes had leaned forward with each and every word he uttered into the phone, ensuring Moss understood that this was far from over. It was hard to relinquish the fury that had embraced him on this tirade. He forced himself to stand and move the damp strands of hair away from his face so that he could see if Brody had been successful with the trace.

Coen finally gave him the thumbs up in success.

"I must admit that I didn't believe you of all people would make such a challenging adversary." It was more than apparent that Townes had taken Moss by surprise in bringing Caroline Marinovic into the conversation. It was a slight victory compared to what was to come. Unfortunately, Moss once again turned the tables. "There will be no more hunt. At least, not in this life. I'll make sure Shailyn knows that you're still trying to avenge her honor."

"What are you talking about, Moss? Are you going to make this easy on me?"

Coen had already set the receiver down in its cradle and was making his way toward the door to join the others in their preparation to leave the compound when he turned on the heel of his boot. They both stood still as Townes listened to Moss' shocking response.

"Merry Christmas, Mr. Calvert. I'm sure we'll meet again, seeing as hell is certain for us both."

For a brief moment, Townes thought Moss had disconnected the line. That was until a loud explosion ripped through the connection to the point where Townes had to take the cell phone away from his ear. Only then was there complete silence.

Townes continued to stare at the phone as he finally understood the meaning of Moss' words. Were they genuine? Had Moss gone and done them all a favor?

"Have Brody get that helicopter back up in the air immediately." Townes gave the directive, but he wasn't celebrating just yet. "I think Moss might have just done us a courtesy of sorts."

CHAPTER SEVEN

"IT'S GETTING LATE. Why don't you head over to the main house? I'll let you know if we receive word from the team."

Shailyn continued to chew on her thumbnail, her success in kicking the disgusting habit crumbling as the afternoon progressed. What if Moss had in fact killed himself? What would happen then? Would she go back into WITSEC because of the other psychopathic sycophants Moss had waiting in the wings to fulfill his demented destiny or could she finally reclaim her life and live in peace?

There would be no answers to those questions until they had confirmation that Moss was well and truly gone from this world. It was very likely that Moss was merely using his own exact gambit to reveal theirs as a sham.

"Shailyn?"

She looked away from one of the computer monitors displaying an online newsfeed from one of the local stations broadcasting live from the scene of a massive explosion in a remote section of a secluded area. Brody was regarding her with a peaked level of concern, but he didn't know that she was an insomniac. She couldn't just go to sleep like everyone else. What he could understand was her fervent need to confirm Moss' death.

"I'm fine," Shailyn replied with a small smile of reassurance offered up to ease his concern. The bright colors of his Hawaiian shirt were out of place in a situation like this, but she'd been told by Remy that it was a staple of his everyday wardrobe. The woman was clearly in love with the man despite the floral shirts, and vice versa. Shailyn and Remy had been introduced shortly after her arrival. It had been nice to have some female company that wasn't some kind of hard-nosed federal agent. It wouldn't surprise her if that was short-lived. She was used to leaving people behind with little to no warning. "Do you believe that Moss took his own life? The monster was in love with himself."

Brody didn't reply to her question right away. Instead, he focused on some satellite images that didn't appear to be in real time. It was evident that the highly-detailed photographs were of the same area prior to the explosion, but he kept swapping back and forth between those and real-time images.

She quickly glanced up to the main overhead monitor displaying the smoldering cabin that had clearly burnt to the ground. The visual wasn't the best given the distance, but it was sharp enough to convey the impression that there was nothing left but ashes on the ground at the site of where an old swamper's cabin had been.

"I believe Moss is highly intelligent, and we can't bank on any results until the DNA from whatever body found onsite is matched to what we have on file for Moss." Brody clicked through some more images as he sipped coffee out of a white porcelain mug. His actions were that of a man settling in for a long night. "Unfortunately, that could take days to confirm."

"What are you doing?"

Shailyn leaned in close as she wrapped her arms around her waist. She studied the monitor, still not sure of what Brody could possibly be looking for. He finally pointed to the images that seemed to be stacking up on top of each other as he continued to click through them.

"These pictures were taken by a reconnaissance aircraft a couple of hours before the explosion. We covered the entire area over the past few days. I'm looking through each picture we have of that same area to see if Moss appears on any of them. Actually, I'm searching for anyone who had been in the vicinity of the cabin." Brody set his mug down on what looked to be some kind of new-aged coaster. There was a cord connecting the metal disc to one of the monitors. This place was full of weird gadgets, but her interest lay elsewhere. "It would be an easier way to prove Moss wasn't inside the structure when the explosion occurred."

The door to the outbuilding opened to reveal Remy and Brettany. It had been so nice to see her friend from her childhood, but they hadn't had enough time to talk after being told of Moss' phone call to Townes. There wasn't much Shailyn could say in her defense that Moss had chosen to bring Brett into this sick and twisted game he was still playing with all their lives.

"Hey," Brett greeted softly, slipping farther into Brody's domain. There were computer monitors covering every square inch of what looked to be a custom designed desk. It was hard for Shailyn to tear her eyes away from the images Brody was painstakingly taking his time combing through in his quest to spot Moss. "We brought you something to eat."

"Oh, I'm not—"

All three of them turned to give her disbelieving and stern looks at her most recent attempt at denying sustenance. Yes, she was already on the thin side…but living in constant fear had a way of doing that to a person. Remy held up a tray that appeared to be two servings of soup and an assortment of sandwiches. It was quite odd for her to have someone concerned with whether or not she ate dinner. She'd been on her own for a very long time.

"Thank you," Shailyn murmured, taking a seat in one of the rolling chairs and adjusting the scarf she'd tied around her neck. It was odd that there was a small Christmas tree on a table near the back of the room. Nothing that had occurred lately coincided with the spirit of Christmas. "It smells delicious."

The weather in Florida was too hot and humid for her to wear her standard turtleneck in an attempt to cover her scars. She had quite a few of them that were impossible to hide otherwise, so she compromised with a semi-opaque white scarf. There were times over the years where she'd had to make such purchases, but she had learned early on to make sure the fabric was soft. The nerve damage made it hard to tolerate any other type of material that would chafe.

The same went for sleeves on the blouses or other tops she owned. She always wore long sleeves, and today was no different than any other day. It was rather easy to do considering she was almost always in air-conditioned buildings. The white shirt she currently wore lay nicely over her collarbone, almost meeting the matching scarf so that no skin could be visible.

"Is there anything else we can get you?" Brett asked, sharing a look of concern with Remy. Once again, Shailyn found it odd that she had to justify her mental and physical health. "You've had a really long night and day. You must be exhausted by now."

"Honestly, I'm not tired." Shailyn indicated that Brett and Remy should both join her. Talking to them might keep her from finding a vehicle and driving out to the area where Townes and the rest of his team had gone for confirmation regarding Moss' death. Sitting here and doing nothing had her itching to do anything useful. "How are your parents?"

"Let's just say that they're not happy that I'm here instead of back in Colorado where they can keep an eye on me," Brett replied with half-smile and a shrug.

Shailyn was wise enough not to ask about the past few weeks Brett had endured regarding the loss of not one, but two friends who'd gotten caught up in an affair gone wrong. It hadn't helped to brighten their reunion when Moss had slipped his slithering hand into the mix all because Shailyn and Brett had once been close childhood friends.

In the end, all this destruction fell at Shailyn's damaged feet. Moss had left a trail of bodies for her to follow.

Brett and Remy carried the disjointed conversation while Brody continued to work and Shailyn thought over the last thirty-six or so hours. She had never expected to set eyes on Townes Calvert again, let alone be staying under his roof as if they were long lost friends.

He wasn't anything like the man she'd met and become infatuated with years ago. He'd become somewhat mysterious. There were additional layers to his personality that shined through the house he'd built on acres and acres of land that offered a peaceful existence dressed up as an armed fortress. It was unlike the simple existence they'd both experienced earlier in their lives.

Shailyn found herself wanting to know more about the man he'd become, but she'd had to remind herself that this stay was only temporary. Whether or not Moss was truly discovered dead among the ruins of that cabin, her future most likely held the same monotonous routine as it had before in WITSEC—living under an assumed name in a random town chosen by the good folks within the program. She would do well to remember that her life was not her own.

"This could all be over soon." Brett was so optimistic in her statement. Shailyn didn't have the heart to tell her it really didn't matter if Moss was dead or not. Nothing really changed…did it? "You can have your life back, Shailyn."

"Exactly how does that happen?" Shailyn asked warily, instantly wishing she'd remained silent. Asking questions no one knew the answer to would get them nowhere.

Shailyn and Brody shared a look that had her accepting her fate. There would be no friendships started here that would last, nor would there be old ones renewed. She couldn't allow herself to know the man on the white horse. It didn't matter that the dragon was slain. The end result would be the same. She would continue her existence alone.

"It depends." Brody must have finished searching through the various images the recon flight had provided him, because he cleared them off the monitor. The other online news channel still showed the burning embers under artificial light brought in by the fire marshals or forensics. He turned on his stool and met her accepting gaze. "Shailyn might do well to consider staying in the WITSEC program, thus protecting herself from wannabes or those simply looking to finish what Moss started."

"You mean she wouldn't get her life back?" Remy was already shaking her head in disagreement with that version of the story. The pretty blonde was still wearing the business suit she'd had on earlier. She was straightening out her lapels as if she were ready to do battle. Shailyn experienced a sadness that the two of them most likely wouldn't become friends. "That makes no sense. The threat is neutralized. What are the chances that some other unrelated whackjob would even venture getting close to Shailyn? Besides, you said that would be one consideration. That would mean she *could* reclaim the life that's been taken from her."

"What kind of life would she have as Shailyn Doyle,

though?" Brett asked skeptically, scrunching her nose as she listed possible scenarios. "The media would hound her relentlessly for months, looking for any kind of angle on an old story. Unless that is beneficial to the process of putting this whole thing behind her. I mean, no one would dare go near her if she's being monitored twenty-four-seven."

Shailyn was only too happy to lean back in her chair and allow them to discuss her future as if she wasn't there. It prevented her from having to answer. Not to mention that she didn't want to reply, because she was still too afraid of believing that the monster who'd dragged her into the darkness filled with nothing but pain could actually be gone from this earth without so much as a thunderclap.

It was sad, in a way. Not even Shepherd Moss' death could erase the scars he'd left behind on people's lives.

Shailyn would forever carry with her his mark of evil.

DARKNESS SURROUNDED HIM, *but all he had to do now was look for the light.*

Shailyn would be waiting for him.

CHAPTER EIGHT

TOWNES PAUSED IN front of Shailyn's bedroom door, contemplating waking her. Roughly a day and a half had passed since his brief exchange with Moss. He'd spent nearly half his time at the crime scene where the body was discovered in the middle of some godforsaken woods, overgrown with pine trees and scrub brush.

The cabin had been where Catherine Marinovic's body had been unearthed accidently a short distance from a hiking trail. The woods around this area of Florida were thick with ticks, chiggers, and what he thought of as the state bird—mosquitoes. God knows why the hikers decided to dig their fire pit at the exact spot, but the skull they'd uncovered had sure made an impression. Of that he was sure.

The exhaustion of the extensive site search had finally caught up with him, and yet he couldn't share with her anything she probably didn't already know.

Everything pointed toward Moss taking his own life a short distance from the very place his killing desires had emerged. Unfortunately, no changes would be made to their current investigation without verification. Shailyn Doyle would remain dead to the rest of the world until forensics confirmed it was Shepherd Moss' body who lay in the ashes of the ruined cabin.

He quietly entered his own room. The adjacent private bathroom offered him the luxury of a quick shower. He didn't linger under the hot spray of water, nor did he bother grabbing a pair of briefs as he passed through his dressing room. He preferred to sleep in the nude, anyway.

He wasn't ashamed of the multitude of scars crisscrossing his body. He looked upon life as a battle. Wounds were merely the result of joining the fight.

He finally brought his hand down over the light switch before entering his suite. Sleep was only a few steps away.

"Was it Moss?"

Townes instinctively made sure the towel around his waist was secured. Shailyn had caught him off guard, and he chalked up his surprise due to his level of exhaustion.

She stood next to the window where she'd apparently raised the security shutter to look outside. Brody mentioned she had a penchant for doing so when they debriefed.

Shailyn was dressed as if she were ready to start her day in a long-sleeved, thin black top and matching scarf. The material appeared smooth by the looks of it. A pair of white jeans were complemented by her dark socks, though she wasn't wearing any shoes. She had her arms wrapped around her waist as she stared out over the pond at the back of the property.

"I'm sure Brody already explained to you that we'll need to wait for confirmation from the DNA samples taken at the crime scene by the State Forensics Lab technicians. The FBI took samples, as well. I'm sure one of them will have some results in a couple days." Townes glanced over at his dresser before settling his gaze on her once more. She must have turned on his bedside lamp when he'd been in the shower. The wattage was low, but the golden hue was enough to make out her beautiful features. "Why don't you turn in for the night? There's nothing any of us can do at the moment."

"I didn't get to tell you in Portland, but I should have made it clear that my father had no right to turn you away. It wasn't your fault." Shailyn tilted her head back as if she could scream in frustration, but she composed herself enough that she was able to face him with a small smile of regret. "It would have been nice if you'd been by my side throughout the ordeal of the trial."

"I *was* by your side."

Townes didn't want to rehash past events. Nothing they said or did could ever change the paths they'd taken since the night that she'd gone missing.

"You know that's not what I meant," Shailyn murmured, her soft sigh somehow reverberating off the walls. "Would you have—"

"Don't." Townes lived with a lot of regret. He wouldn't stand here and have either one of them play the *what if* game. "The only thing that matters is the outcome of the DNA analysis."

"You and I both know that the results will change nothing for me." Shailyn slowly shook her head at the impossible situation she still faced. "You could have just as easily left me in Maine. The U.S. Marshals Service could have explained the plan you put into place, left me to my anonymity, and the events that have followed would have still unfolded in the same manner. Why am I here, Townes?"

He ran a hand through his damp strands in an attempt to curb his frustration. Every single thing she said rang true, with the exception of him making sure of her security.

This fortress he'd built had been constructed with her safety in mind. The outer perimeter had antipersonnel movement sensors and cameras. They were laid out in overlapping grids to provide redundancy in the system. GPS-enabled sensor suites were strewn throughout the property so that any movement could be pinpointed to the inch, which included IR sensors that could detect a human heartbeat within twenty-five yards.

Brody had designed the relational position resolution algorithms, leaving him the ability to locate the exact position of an intruder approaching the house in real time as they ran within one meter anywhere on the grounds.

The security system on the surrounding property was nothing compared to the integrated systems managed by specifically designed software that safeguarded this house.

All outside access doors were made with steel casements stuck into the thick log walls. The doors themselves were either steel-plated with bulletproof glass or solid core. The shutters over all the windows could resist automatic .30 caliber rifle fire.

The alarm systems had two hardline connections and dual cell backups with an emergency satellite connection. The compound was manned by twenty heavily armed sentries, though no one on the outside would ever notice their presence.

Every building on the property had an emergency generator backup power and dedicated circuits for their security systems. All the air management units had active carbon filters and secured clean air intakes to guard against gas attacks. The water was drawn from an underground cistern and ran through an ionizer to burn off any foreign contaminants before being purified with an RO filter structure. All the overlapping security systems were firewalled and monitored onsite as well as recorded twenty-four-seven.

And he'd done all this for her.

Townes refused to stand here and answer her question, because that would mean revealing just how selfish a man he really was. He'd always wanted to see her one more time. No, he had *needed* to see her with his own two eyes so that he could reassure himself that they'd made all the right decisions so many years ago.

"Shailyn, your safety is my first and only priority." Townes walked across the room to where his dresser was against the far wall. He opened to the top drawer and removed a pair of black briefs. She wouldn't appreciate being treated with kid gloves, so he purposefully dropped the towel before stepping into them and pulling up the elastic waistband. He leaned down to pick up the towel before tossing it on the end of the bed. He retraced his steps back across the room to secure the security shutter before providing his answer. "Moss can't reach you while you're on this property. I've made sure of that. As to your earlier declaration, his death would give you choices, but they are few and far between."

"There are only two choices of which I know are laid out for me, but neither one are too appealing." The proximity of Shailyn's voice told him that she was closer than she'd been before. "I can go back into WITSEC, or I can reclaim my life and risk attack by his followers. Both have more cons than pros, in my opinion. I'd rather die in the light than disappear into the dark."

Townes removed the towel from the bed and hung it up in the bathroom. He walked back into the room and opened the lower drawer of the dresser, retrieving a pair of jeans. He wasn't ready to fully discuss her options. There was still quite a bit that needed to take place before deciding on an outcome.

"I wouldn't stress over a decision that might not need to be made should we discover that Moss is still kicking." Townes pulled the jeans up to his waist, leaving the button unfastened. He figured he'd be shedding the denim soon enough after she'd left his room. He needed to get some sleep before he said or did something he couldn't take back. "I wouldn't put it past him to have created this diversion just to spite us. He could very well be watching the reactions of the media, the feds, and SSI. The best thing you can do right now is rest. Take it a day at a time and watch as the information rolls in."

Shailyn hadn't crossed the room to the door as he'd assumed she would, but instead made her way to the end of the bed. He still held the waist of his jeans with a hand on his hip. He was at a loss as to what she expected of him at this hour of the night.

"You're evading my question."

"Yes," Townes answered truthfully. She wasn't ready to hear why he'd brought her here, just as he wasn't ready to reveal his genuine motives. "I am."

Shailyn regarded him with those emerald green eyes of hers that held no fire the way they once did. When was the last time she'd truly smiled? Did she ever laugh anymore? The slight blemishes underneath her lower lashes were a telltale sign that she didn't get enough sleep. The urge to take care of her was overwhelming.

"How many hours of sleep do you get a night?"

Townes didn't expect her to respond right away. Her pride had always gotten the best of her. She refused to admit defeat. It was the reason she was alive.

Shailyn glanced toward the door, but there was something in her expression that made him believe she didn't want to be alone. Honestly, he was surprised given that it was something she was most likely used to in the years she'd been in the WITSEC program. Her file gave no indication she'd made any friends or even new acquaintances.

As a gentleman, he shouldn't even be contemplating what was going through his mind, but that didn't stop him from brushing past her. The warmth of her skin was like a strong enticement that he would have to ignore for now. He tossed his hands in the air with more force than necessary, but the small exaggerated movement allowed him time to rein himself in before he said something he'd rather not. She had to know that he was frustrated.

Townes had taken off his holster upon entering his bedroom and set it on his nightstand, but he took the time to sling the leather strap over the corner of the headboard. It made for an easy draw in the middle of the night, if necessary. He then pulled the dark brown comforter down to reveal luxury ivory French linen custom printed sheets he'd had shipped from D. Porthault in Paris. The material resembled the emerald green herringbone pattern of a palm frond. The extremely fine thread count made for an exceptionally comfortable night's sleep, which they both desperately needed.

"What are you doing?"

"Catching what sleep I can before all hell breaks loose in a few hours." Townes settled back against his pillow, only to realize that he'd forgotten his hair tie. He realized that the rebellion against cutting his hair had something to do with rejoining civilian life, but he didn't bother to psychoanalyze all that crap to death. There was no changing who he was after all these years. "You're more than welcome to join me if you want to sleep."

Townes reached for the black tie he used to pull his hair back with and quickly made use of the elastic band. He lifted his arms up and linked his fingers behind his head before once again closing his eyes. He'd managed to catch Shailyn's parted lips in her disbelief that he was all but ending this conversation. She didn't seem to comprehend that nothing they said or did given the current situation could rush the results of the DNA tests or press the discovery of Moss' current predicament.

"A few hours of sleep, Shailyn," Townes muttered, listening

closely for any sign that she was walking toward the door. "Nothing more."

He would have easily said that three to four minutes had passed before he heard the rustling of her clothes as she walked. She wasn't taking them off, by any means, but she was making her way closer to the bed. The mattress dipped slightly, though it was hard to register seeing as she didn't weigh all that much. He couldn't say that he wasn't surprised by her decision to stay. Hell, she'd already dressed for the day as it was.

"Don't. Please."

Townes had been in the process of reaching for the bedside lamp when her directive stopped him cold. He recalled reading in the Marshal's daily reports over the last four months that she left the majority of the lights on in her house during the evening hours. The details didn't include specific rooms, though he was now considering narrowing the scope of those reports. It would have been beneficial to know she slept with the lights on.

"Come here."

"Maybe I should—"

Townes didn't wait for her to finish that sentence. She looked damned uncomfortable with her ankles crossed, her body stiff as a board, and her arms crossed over her middle. He couldn't take it, and he sure as hell couldn't sleep knowing that she was running over scenarios in her mind as if it were a race. He wrapped his hand around her wrist and drew her close.

"Close your eyes, freckles." Townes winced when he let her nickname slip past his lips. That was nothing compared to when her soft cheek rested against his chest. The difference in temperatures was striking. She'd been cold to the touch on the airplane, but he was coming to think it was a constant thing. "Get some rest."

Townes lifted his left arm up behind his head, not wanting

to crowd her as she struggled with her decision to stay. Every muscle in her body was taut with her flight response. He rested his right hand lightly on her hip so that his touch barely registered.

Would she stay?

Five minutes, ten minutes, and then twenty minutes passed until she finally tucked her hand underneath her chin. Little by little, she relaxed against him. The last time he'd held her this close had been after they'd made love the night before she'd been taken and they'd gotten into one hell of an argument. That foolish battle of pride had led her to join her friends at the nightclub where both of their lives had changed course forever.

Townes wanted nothing more than to stroke the silken strands of her hair that had fallen over his arm. He would have liked nothing better than to shift so that he was above her, kissing her and making love to her the way she deserved, as they had once taken for granted. Yet he was well aware of how truly blessed he was to have her by his side at this very moment.

Another thirty minutes passed when her breathing evened out, telling him that she'd fallen into a light sleep. He didn't move. He stayed exactly where he was so that he didn't disturb her rest. It seemed that he would have to go without, but he wouldn't have it any other way.

CHAPTER NINE

*S*HE DIDN'T WANT *to open her eyes. He would still be there, standing above her with that vile smile. Her tongue was bleeding from her attempt to keep from screaming in agony. The strangled sound emitting from her throat seemed to increase his vigor. She wouldn't satisfy his thirst to hear her fear. She refused to give him what he wanted.*

"He can't save you."

Shailyn bolted upright, immediately closing her eyes against the sunshine pouring in through the windows. That telltale sign told her instantly she wasn't home in the WITSEC safe house.

She brought up her knees and rested her elbows against the white denim as she pressed her palms against her forehead. Even, measured breaths finally brought her heartrate under control from the nightmare.

Something was different.

Shailyn finally lowered her hands and let them dangle in front of her as she searched Townes' bedroom. What was bothering her? He wasn't inside the room, nor was he in the bathroom. She would have sensed his presence, but that wasn't what troubled her.

A quick glance at the clock on his bedside table revealed that it was closing in on seven thirty in the morning. She quickly calculated the time and realized that she had to have slept for close to four hours.

Was it possible that estimate was right?

Shailyn inhaled deeply, trying to clear the cobwebs. All she managed to do was capture Townes' comforting, yet intoxicating, scent. She never should have stayed here in his room. All last night had done was make her want something that she couldn't have, which made it even more desirable.

She had almost walked out of his bedroom upon seeing him in nothing but a towel wrapped around his waist last night. He used to always take his clothes into the bathroom with him when they were together in the past. She suspected a lot of things had changed since then, but that didn't mean she wasn't taken aback at the sight of his build. His large frame was even more solid now, with his muscles contoured in places she longed to retrace.

The black eagle globe and anchor tattoo on his neck stood out even more against the stark white towel. It appeared even larger and somehow gave him an air of lethality. Having him near her mistakenly conveyed a belief that she could face anything. He was merely a man. He was definitely an imposing warrior, but not a Norse God. She would do well to remember the mistakes of her past.

Townes' dark brown hair had still been damp when he appeared out of the bathroom. The wet strands had been combed back from his face, revealing the two-inch scar along his jawline in more detail. How many times had she kissed that wound to belay his own distant fears?

She had never expected the sweet pain of lost love to shoot through her as she rested her cheek gently on his chest. The wistful memories had all but drowned her with their return. The comfort and security he offered had been like drinking fresh water directly from the hand pump of a cool well after having spent the day in the fields baling fresh hay and breathing nothing but dust.

It was upon that moment she realized just how painful it was to her heart being back in his consuming presence, knowing full well they would be taking separate paths once again when her case finally came to a close.

The urge to write in her journal was overwhelming, and most likely the reason she had awoken with such a start. She finally figured out what was disturbing her this morning. It was then she realized what was truly bothering her. The remnants of last night's nightmare weren't based on memories. Shepherd Moss had never uttered those words to her—*he can't save you.*

Shailyn fought the nausea that suddenly hit her stomach. She swung her legs over the right side of the bed, but didn't immediately stand. What did it mean that her dreams were changing? Had it been a premonition? A sign?

"Good morning."

Shailyn swung her gaze to the entrance of the bedroom, surprised to find Townes standing in the middle of the open doorway. She hadn't heard the clicking of the latch or noticed the door swinging inward in her struggle to understand her dream.

"Morning," Shailyn replied softly, not wanting him to ask her any questions.

She never had the intention of falling asleep last night. All she'd wanted was to have company while they awaited the results of the DNA analysis. He didn't need to see her grapple with her nightmares, and she was thankful of his absence when those troubling visions had arrived.

"I brought you some coffee. It's most likely going to be a long day."

"Here I thought you had the power to shorten our wait," Shailyn said lightly, grateful when he didn't make this moment uncomfortable. "Is that bacon I smell?"

"Brett is making breakfast as we speak and wondering if you'd like to join them in the kitchen."

Townes' grey eyes darkened when her fingers brushed his as she took the mug from his hand. Memories of other mornings like this flooded her mind, but she let them wash away like faded recollections tended to do. She would still have to leave this sanctuary, no matter the outcome. Eventually the time would come.

"Here." Townes stepped forward and reached for her scarf. Shailyn involuntarily tried to take a step back, but the bed stopped her progress. Had he not taken ahold of her wrist to steady the mug, she had no doubt the coffee would have spilled over the rim and burned her skin. "I'm only adjusting the material, Shailyn. You have no reason to fear me."

She refused to meet his gaze. No one could understand the disgust that overwhelmed her every single time she looked in the mirror. Moss had not left a few scars behind, but hundreds of individual marks. He even carved the date he'd thought she would die from her wounds underneath her right breast.

He was evil all the way down to his core. He enjoyed each and every movement of the blade and its impact he'd left on her body. He relished the blue tip of the torch searing her flesh to seal the bleeding. It allowed him to start over again and again and again.

"Look at me."

Townes uttered those words in a manner she'd never heard before. She complied, but only because he surprised her with the firm directive. He gradually pulled the material down far enough to reveal one of the longer scars on her neck, never once breaking eye contact with her. She hadn't realized she'd been holding her breath until he ever so slowly leaned down and gently pressed his lips against the bane of her existence to the very manifestation of evil left on her soul.

He pulled back before she ever had the chance to react. Both of his hands now cupped her face so that she had no choice but to stare directly into those grey eyes that had haunted her just as much as her fears.

"You are just as beautiful now as the day I met you, freckles."

And just like that…he took his leave.

Townes walked away and through the door as if he'd been nothing but an apparition.

Shailyn lifted her arm and pressed her right hand against the fresh searing sensation he'd left on her flesh. There were so many things left unsaid between the two of them, but he'd made it so that neither one had to say a word. It was as if they were back when they'd started out together, only they were still on that same collision course that would have them reliving the past with the very monster who had driven the wedge between them.

Shailyn set her coffee down on the nightstand when she finally composed herself to adjust her scarf. If Brett were in the kitchen, then that meant the majority of others would be in attendance as well. She didn't waste time, wondering if they would receive word today on the DNA analysis of the body left behind in the ruins of the cabin.

The news confirming Shepherd Moss' death wouldn't completely change her life, but it would make it easier to join the living.

Low murmurs of conversations could be heard coming up from the kitchen as she slowly descended the stairs. There was lighted garland strung between the spindles. She'd caught sight of a massive Christmas tree in the living room upon arriving. Someone had taken time to decorate Townes' residence for the holidays. Had he done it in what little spare time he had these days, or had one of his many guests taken it upon him or herself to bring some cheer to the massive house?

A round of good mornings greeted her, but those words didn't come from as many as she'd envisioned sitting around the table. There were still a few of the team members missing.

Brett was serving up what appeared to be blueberry pancakes and bacon on several plates positioned in a row on the counter. Ashlyn, Keane's fiancée, was standing off to the side with her phone pressed against her ear. Remy was nowhere to be seen, and Cailyn was sitting at the table jotting down something or another in a notebook.

The paper and pen caused Shailyn to think of her own journal and the fact that she hadn't recorded the alteration of her dreams. She mentally created a to-do list in her mind. A shiver of unease traveled down her spine at the thought she'd had some sort of premonition, but that wouldn't come true if they could only confirm it was Moss' body they'd uncovered in the ashes.

"Eat. You'll need your energy."

Shailyn startled at the command given by Townes, who'd magically appeared behind her. She didn't have to turn to look at him as he quietly walked across the kitchen tile to pour himself a fresh cup of coffee from the community pot. He was wearing his usual pair of jeans and a black faded t-shirt that no longer had a recognizable decal on the back to determine its origin.

"Royce and Keane are due to call in with a SITREP in ten minutes," Sawyer said, picking up two plates while flashing a wry smile at Brett in appreciation. He set the meals down on the table, joining Camryn, to whom Shailyn had yet to be formally introduced. The beautiful actress had lifted a hand in greeting. "Brody's setting things up now."

"We'll need to patch in Agent Gordon. Brody is most likely

establishing the protocols for the FBI technicians to follow." Townes replaced the glass carafe on the burner before leaning back against the counter. He was so at ease with these people, unlike he'd been with her crowd of friends or family back in the day. "I gave him my word we'd keep him apprised of the investigation."

"Morning." The single word was more mumbled than spoken clearly as Coen walked into the kitchen from the patio door. His dark gaze landed immediately on Brett, who was already leaning over the counter for a good morning kiss. "Brody paid me twenty bucks to bring him a plate."

"Brett, you're going to cause all of us to gain at least ten pounds this month if you keep dishing up this kind of chow." Townes stole a piece of bacon before Brett could stop him. She shot Coen a look of amusement. "I might have to open a Colorado branch just so Coen…"

The conversation faded from Shailyn's awareness as she thought back to when she and Townes had been together. No one had truly known of their relationship, and it was even kept under the radar during the trial. Her friends had been aware her father had hired him as added protection, though most of them had given him a wide berth due to his rough appearance and formidability. He never seemed to care what others thought of him, but the interaction with his team as if they were family gave her yet another perspective.

A picture of herself caught her eye on the small flat screen nestled in the corner of the counter. It was so unexpected that she took an involuntary step forward to read the caption on the bottom of the news report.

"Would you please turn the volume up?" Shailyn asked Ashlyn as the other woman disconnected her call.

"…when the news broke. Dr. Carter Doyle had this to say in

speaking with our own Maura Jane of TV Nine News."

"We're heartbroken. This isn't how we envisioned spending our Christmas…mourning our only daughter." It was easy to catch the hitch in her father's voice. Tears filled her eyes upon realizing the pain he and her mother must be experiencing, yet there was a distance between them that made this surreal. It was as if she were a million miles away. "The U.S. Marshals Service gave us the courtesy of telling my wife and I in private, but then to hear about the possible death of Shepherd Moss today was a blow neither of us expected. I hope he rots in the deepest pit of hell."

"Ashlyn." Townes only had to say the woman's name. She turned off the television, allowing the kitchen to descend into silence. "Shailyn, would you like to join us for the conference call?"

Shailyn had to swallow a couple of times before she was able to speak clearly.

"What do you hope to hear from Royce and Keane?" Shailyn set her coffee on the edge of the counter, never having taken a sip. The bitter drink would only add to her nausea. "Are they still at the cabin searching the area?"

"Not exactly." Townes walked around Brett and reached for one of the plates. He pushed it across the island in front of the last stool. He nodded to indicate she should take a seat. "Once you eat some breakfast, we'll head over to the team room."

Shailyn could see that he wasn't going to budge unless she'd taken a few bites of breakfast. She almost protested, but there were too many eyes watching her every move. She didn't want to make a scene, so she quietly took a seat and picked up her fork.

"I'd like to be prepared for what they have to say, Townes."

Her quiet statement caught his attention, and he finally nodded his understanding.

"Keane and Royce drove into town to speak with Lucas Grove." Shailyn recognized the name as that of Caroline Marinovic's fiancé. She wasn't sure what she expected Townes to say about the man who most likely lost the love of his life to a monster, but it certainly wasn't the words that might very well mean Moss was still out there somewhere. "He's gone missing, Shailyn. His friends and family haven't seen him in two weeks. He could very well be the body we found at the cabin."

HE WATCHED FROM afar as pandemonium settled over the small town.

The townsfolk had no idea what was going on other than the charred body left at the cabin might be him or Lucas Grove. Won't the authorities be surprised to find the identity didn't match either one?

It was Townes Calvert's reaction he wished to see most.

He slipped his free hand into the pocket of his slacks as he used the rim of his to-go cup from the local coffee shop to camouflage his face. It wouldn't do to have one of the residents recognize him after all the trouble he'd gone to set up such an elaborate ruse.

Would Calvert make the connection, or would he slip and finally show his hand?

The anger that had initially shadowed his mind with doubts had slowly dissipated. He would know if Shailyn were gone from this world. He'd known it when Caroline had crossed over, and Shailyn's passing would be no different.

CHAPTER TEN

"WHO DECORATED YOUR house?"

Townes glanced up from the reports he'd been looking over covering all known details of Caroline Marinovic's murder. Brody had compiled the information from multiple agencies. Shailyn no longer resembled the brunette he remembered now that she'd gone back to her natural auburn tresses. The light dusting of freckles was covered by a light application of makeup, but there was no mistaking the lack of color in her cheeks as she didn't use that much blush.

"You're going to have to clarify your question. Your assumption that I consider it my house is a bit off, though. The entire team has a home here, so I consider it *our* home." Townes leaned back in his office chair, thinking to himself that Shailyn belonged here as well. She most likely wouldn't agree, but it was a bridge he would cross when the time was right. He motioned for her to take the guest chair, but instead she ran her hand along one of the bookshelves as she studied the leather-bound classics he'd acquired over the years. "Are you asking about the interior design of the house or the festive Christmas decorations?"

Townes waited patiently for her reply, sensing she didn't want to be having this small talk about earth tones or holiday garland. Lucas Grove was still missing, the DNA analysis on the body found in the burnt ruins of the cabin had yet to be revealed, and the various authorities were basically in limbo until either the team turned up a lead or the local or FBI labs came through with the results.

"I guess both." Shailyn tucked a strand of those red tresses he'd grown to love watching her day in and day out in the courtroom. She'd been a brunette the day he'd met her, but this rustic shade suited her much better. He never once looked upon her as a victim. Her strength shone through every word documented in the trial transcripts. "I thought this place was going to be like all the other safe houses I've seen over the years. You were pretty adamant about not settling down back in the day. In fact, at the time you wouldn't buy anything that wouldn't fit in the back of your pick-up or in the trailer with your bike. I remember you saying as much."

"Age and wisdom play a very important part in determining what's important."

Townes had removed his hair tie earlier when a tension headache had started to take hold. He didn't hesitate to grab the elastic band and secure the strands at the base of his neck. He stayed where he was, though. It wouldn't take long before she brought up the real reason she had entered his domain.

"I have very particular tastes when it comes to my living quarters. I tend toward the more practical side." Townes reached for the white porcelain mug he'd just topped off with his personal machine. "I was here close to a year putting the finishing touches on this place before I brought in the team. They all have their own apartments or houses either in the city or the surrounding towns. I've been having them stay here mostly because of the personal attack Moss made on Camryn. It wasn't much of a stretch to believe he'd target the other team members and their families. Some of the men had stayed here when it was convenient rather than running back to their places prior to the team and their loved ones becoming a target."

Shailyn had moved to the bookshelf that contained framed pictures of when he'd been in the service. Unfortunately, some of the men in those photographs hadn't returned home on their own two feet. He honored them by remembering their faces and the sacrifices they made in his own way. He believed that he kept them forever young in his mind by remembering how they lived their lives and the tribulations that they had all endured together.

"How can you simply sit here as if nothing is happening outside of your little fort?" And there it was. Shailyn's frustration and anger at being helpless was now beginning to show, and he didn't blame her in the least. It wasn't easy considering all the facts, yet remaining behind to shoulder the burden. She dropped her hand from the shelf and turned to face him in aggravation. "You should be out looking for Lucas Grove."

"Keane, Royce, Sawyer, and Coen are tracking down leads, interviewing family and friends of Caroline Marinovic and Lucas Grove. I hired them for a reason. They have to be my eyes and ears on the ground." Townes rolled back his desk chair enough so that he could cross his ankle over his knee. He took a drink of his coffee, needing her to see that he wasn't allowing the wait to get to him. She would react to his lead. At least, he hoped. "I also have other Marshals out there following up on incidental interviews and heading up the aerial search of the county and subsequent areas where Moss may have fled to if he's still alive. Just to make it perfectly clear, I'm not leaving you here alone."

Townes' last statement caught her attention, and she wisely refrained from commenting. He'd given her enough indications of what he desired for their future that he might as well have spelled it out for her in writing. It had taken him quite a long time to come to terms with the way he'd handled her original protection detail, her father's demands after she recovered, the ensuing trial, her induction into WITSEC participation, and now the fallout of Moss' escape from a federal prison.

Too much time had been wasted by both of them, and he'd already expressed his views on how age and wisdom went hand in hand.

Shailyn would come to him when she was ready to face their past mistakes. He could easily make it so that she didn't have to go back into WITSEC again, providing her around-the-clock personal security even after Moss' demise.

"Do you believe Moss is dead?"

"No, not for one second." Townes stood and pushed the chair back even farther with the back of his knees. "Why don't we head out to the patio? We could both use some fresh air. I have a 2005 Robusto Montecristo Edmundo that has been resting with its brothers in my humidor for the past six months. I believe it's time to liberate one of those sticks."

Shailyn shook her head in answer, once again walking the line of shelves that held two hundred or more of the leather-bound classics. What exactly did she think she'd find?

"I don't believe he's dead either." Shailyn ran a finger over the spines of each book until she came to the corner. The window of his office faced the inner courtyard, so during the day he kept the security shutter raised. The curtains were drawn open, revealing one of his favorite shade trees on the property. The tree was an old cedar with tangled branches that reached for the sky. The cedars weren't the fullest trees, but they all had fine character and that was enough. "Was my father convincing?"

Townes thought he had complete control of this conversation and even the ability to ease her concerns. She'd proven him wrong with just one question.

"Yes, at the time he was," Townes replied rather cautiously, stepping out from behind his desk. He was a mere twelve feet from where she was standing. "I'm truly sorry for what your father and mother must be going through. I didn't make this decision lightly, but their grief has to be real in order to satisfy Moss' observations."

It was entirely possible that Moss had one of his acolytes watching the family for any indication that her death might be a ruse. Hell, it could even be their family doctor, for all they knew.

"You asked me if I believed Moss was dead, and my answer was no. I think he's faking his death in an attempt to bring you out of hiding or to cause one of the agencies involved with the hunt to relax their pursuit. The longer we keep you concealed, the more agitated he's going to become. It's then that he will make the mistake of contacting me once again."

"Did you know that I can't have children after what he did to me?"

It was so rare that Townes was taken by true surprise that he needed a moment to repeat her inquiry in his mind.

"Yes. I read the medical reports."

Townes was truthful in his response. He would never mislead her in any way.

"A part of me is grateful that I'll never have to experience what my parents have from the day I went missing to today." Shailyn left her place by the window and walked over to his favorite chair next to the unlit fireplace. She toed off her shoes and took a seat, curling her legs up underneath her. He was fascinated at how fragile yet resilient she was in facing what had to be her greatest fear. "Another piece of me would give anything to experience that kind of unconditional love to another human being. I'd like to see them before I go back into WITSEC."

Shailyn finally met his gaze, her emerald green eyes holding only acceptance. A sharp slice of anger cut into his gut. He wanted her to fight for what she'd been denied.

"I'll make that happen when the time comes."

His declaration seemed to satisfy her. She curled up in the chair and rested her head on her arm. It appeared she was staying in his office for the duration of the wait.

Townes reclaimed his office chair behind the desk, though he didn't bother to pick up the folder he'd been reading over for the hundredth time. Something settled inside of him at her mere presence. This was where she belonged—not WITSEC.

An hour passed before Remy appeared in his office doorway. Shailyn had drifted off to sleep thirty minutes prior, but it was easy to see it was a restless slumber. Whatever he was needed for could wait.

Something stopped him from sending Remy away, though. He held up a finger for her to wait a second. He quickly grabbed a piece of paper and scribbled down his request. He quietly stood, folding the note in half before walking it over to her.

"Brody wanted you to know he's combed through all the footage," Remy whispered, having caught sight of Shailyn curled up in the chair. "No one entered or exited the cabin for seventy-two hours before the fire. He was able to confirm that with coverage the NRO provided of that general area by the way of a byproduct of other scheduled national asset surveillance. He's going farther back to see when Moss arrived there in order to try and trace his steps backwards."

Townes didn't believe for a moment that Moss was dead, but their hands were tied until he was proven otherwise.

"Would you please do me a favor?" Townes waited for Remy to read his request, a bright smile connecting to her sparkling blue eyes. "I'd like to keep this between us until it's done."

"Of course. I think it's a great idea."

Townes waited for Remy to leave before quietly closing the office door to give them some privacy. It was rare that he did so, but he didn't want Shailyn's sleep disturbed. He silently crossed the room and picked up the soft throw blanket he kept near the ottoman on those rare nights in Florida it became chilly. He carefully covered her legs since she always seemed to be cold nowadays, hoping a little warmth might cause her to sleep more comfortably.

Head back to the cabin and check for a concealed access point in the floor.

He constructed the text and sent it to the team so that whoever was closest to that area could return and do a more thorough search of the cabin now that the embers had cooled somewhat. Granted, they'd had limited access until it was safe to scour through the remains completely. He had no doubt they'd missed some type of trap door that led underground through some escape tunnel. It was the only reasonable explanation for the prolonged lack of movement.

Another forty minutes passed as he sat and watched over Shailyn before his phone vibrated with a reply from Sawyer. It wasn't one he'd expected.

No access point.

"Townes?"

He glanced up from his phone to find that Shailyn was studying him with earnest. She thought he'd gotten the results back from forensics on the DNA sample.

"We haven't received word from the lab yet." Townes could still see slight blemishes underneath her lashes that signified she hadn't had nearly enough rest. He wished he had some type of news that would give her hope this manhunt was coming to an end, but he could only give her the facts. "It's Sawyer. I thought maybe there might be an exit from the cabin we weren't aware of initially."

"And?" Shailyn slowly sat upright in the chair and tightly held the edge of the blanket in the palms of her hands. "Did Sawyer find what you expected?"

"No." Townes still held the belief that Moss had somehow gotten out of the cabin before the structure had been engulfed in flames. Unfortunately, evidence didn't lie. "The body found in the remnants of the ruins might very well be Shepherd Moss' remains."

CHAPTER ELEVEN

SHAILYN STARED OUT over the large pond through the window, watching the slight ripples in the water reflecting the moonlight. She guessed the graceful movements were either from the fish feeding or the frogs avoiding the peacock bass. The crickets were endlessly singing their songs of love and the lightning bugs were happily signaling to one another in the same vein. She pressed her palm to the cool glass, realizing that this was the first time she'd openly stood in front of a window to peer at the outside world at night.

She was relatively sure Brody had noted her opening the security shutter from his computer console against his stern warnings, but the restless part of her soul was in desperate need of soothing.

This estate Townes had built was made up of more than just logs and slabs of concrete. It was a place to find oneself and rediscover peace. She would allow herself amity if they ever received word from the forensics lab. She would have thought spending so much time in WITSEC would have taught her patience. That wasn't the case.

It was going on one o'clock in the morning. Townes had spent the majority of the evening in the team room with Brody. Shailyn would have joined him, but Brett had corralled her out on the back deck. The other women had been gathered around a large glass table with several bottles of wine and a tray of cubed cheese and crackers that Brett had no doubt prepared. The nearby fire pit had several logs alight with the accompanying crackling and popping.

Brett was an elementary school teacher in Colorado on break for the upcoming holiday, but from the conversation it seemed that she was returning to Florida at the beginning of the new year to seek a teaching position nearby. Shailyn experienced a stab of jealousy at the ease of which her friend was able to choose a new path to live her life.

In all honesty, all the women had been so nice and welcoming. She hadn't wanted to come across as ungrateful for all they'd done, so she'd joined them for a few hours of enjoying the season's spirits. The conversation was kept light and she found herself even laughing a time or two at some of the memories Brett had brought up in the numerous discussions. Shailyn couldn't remember a time when she'd had that kind of companionship. It had been rather nice, but she was afraid to soak up too much for fear of missing that friendship in the future.

"Going stir crazy? Cabin fever is quite real."

Shailyn had caught Townes' reflection in the window, so she wasn't startled by his sudden presence. His large frame took up the entire doorframe as if he was the door. His long hair was loose and reminded her of a warrior she'd read in the book *Last of the Mohicans* by James Fenimore Cooper when she was a little girl. He couldn't save her even if he'd been able to slay her dragon. There would always be another Magua in the shadows.

"I've lived alone for so long that going stir crazy shouldn't be a possibility for me." Shailyn turned when she caught sight of an expression on his face she'd never seen before. "What happened?"

"DNA confirms the body in the cabin was in fact Moss."
Townes' jawline firmed after announcing the welcome news, yet
his scar was whiter than before. "The Marshals Service is calling
it."

It was easy to see that Townes didn't believe the evidence.
Wasn't something of that nature scientifically conclusive? Wasn't
that what juries based their verdicts on these days?

Shailyn was almost afraid to breathe for fear he would retract
his statement. He'd yet to follow up on his declaration. Instead,
he seemed to be waiting for some type of reaction from her. She
adjusted her scarf before resting the palm of her hand over her
heart. It was her way of ensuring the vital organ was still beating.

"Agent Gordon and the U.S. Marshals were pretty adamant
during the trial that Shepherd Moss' incarceration or even his
death would never guarantee my safety," Shailyn reminded him
tentatively. She would have given anything for him to disagree
with that original assessment, but he just continued to stand in
the doorway and study her. "This really doesn't change anything
for me, does it?"

"It means that Shepherd Moss can't physically hurt you
anymore, and he was a large chunk of that threat."

Anyone else wouldn't have tagged on the adjective *physically*.
Townes was one of the few people who understood that Moss
would always be a part of her life...mentally and emotionally.
She would also have scars for the rest of her life, but there
would never again be a chance for Moss to add to them.

"Am I being given a new identity and taken to another
state?"

"I'd like you to stay here with us until the end of the year, at
the very least." Townes seemed to relax somewhat when he
leaned against the wooden doorframe. His gorgeous strands
framed the right side of his face. "Being a Special Chief Deputy

U.S. Marshal gives me a little leeway in deciding what comes next for you. I believe it would be to your benefit to remain here while we see what ramifications come from the fallout of Moss' death."

A part of Shailyn wanted Townes to take her away immediately, setting her up in another town under another name before leaving her in peace. She wanted this transfer to be like an old bandage stuck to her skin. Rip it off quick so that the pain wasn't prolonged.

"Am I able to visit my parents?"

Shailyn reconsidered her initial reaction. Sometimes a daughter needed to feel the embrace of her mother.

"Yes, although I will have them brought here to see you for the holidays."

Shailyn took another few steps closer to Townes, sensing that he was leaving something out of his admission regarding Moss. She honestly didn't want to know about his reservations, because that would mean a part of herself would have to remain trapped in the past.

"I'm not sure what the appropriate thing is to do now," Shailyn replied honestly, still sorting out a variety of emotions.

"I think I can take care of that for you." Townes held out his hand, his grey eyes containing a bit of mischief that she hadn't seen since the night he'd brought her a white rose with some strawberry wine. How many years had passed between then and now? "Do you trust me?"

For some reason, the question brought a smile to her face. Her cheeks were stiff at the attempt, but she suffered through it.

"Yes."

There was no need to expand on her answer, though she did gently place her fingers in his. He turned on the heels of his military-issued rough-side-out boots and guided her down the long hallway, down the stairwell, and out the front door. The temperature had dropped quite a bit, although the crickets and frogs were still singing their songs.

Shailyn suppressed a shiver as the cool air met her cheeks. She missed the warmth from the fire pit. She would have brought him up short had she'd seen what was in front of them.

"No."

"I thought you said yes," Townes reminded her, reaching for a white motorcycle helmet. He held it higher, as if that was enough of an enticement to get her to straddle a machine that weighed seven times more than her. "Riding a motorcycle on the open road is nothing short of true freedom. You deserve this, freckles."

There it was again. Her nickname. For some reason, hearing it made all the years in between fade away into the night. A laugh bubbled up from somewhere she didn't even know existed.

"This is crazy. I never rode with you before, so what makes you think I've changed my mind and become suicidal?"

"You never needed to feel the fresh air against your face the way you do tonight, nor needed a reminder that you are alive to enjoy the scents and sounds that this world has provided us." Townes waited patiently for her to take a step forward. "Let me give you what you yearn for. It will free your soul."

Shailyn shook her head even though she closed the distance between them. A small smile graced his lips as he carefully slid the protective gear over her hair until the helmet was in place. His large hands went to work until the strap was secure around her chin. His attentiveness and care for her shined through that lone act.

The second he began to tie his hair back and put on his own helmet was when reality hit her regarding the adventure she was about to take. Going to a doctor's appointment had been the exciting moments before, so this was akin to skydiving off a freight train crossing a massive trestle over a mile-high gorge. Her heartrate accelerated and the palms of her hands became sweaty. She tried to dry them on the white jeans she was wearing, but it wasn't helpful in the least.

"I'm boring. You remember that, right?" Shailyn figured she'd get that out there in case he'd forgotten. "My idea of a fun night is making microwave popcorn and watching those B-rated movies that come on after midnight."

"I'm sure we can still catch one of them on the television when we get back from our ride." Townes shrugged into a black leather jacket, though she did notice that he was still wearing his shoulder holster. He was so solid and his movements so sensual that it gave her pause. She'd gone so long without feeling anything other than fear, she wasn't sure she could process anything else. "Here. Let's get this riding jacket on you. It's getting chilly, and it's only going to be colder on the bike. This will protect you from the wind."

Townes picked up a white leather, form-fitting coat that had been lying on the seat of his motorcycle. It was covered with zippers everywhere. He held it so that all she had to do was slip her arms inside. The inside material was slick and rather warm, but it was when he slowly drew the zipper up toward her chin that she recognized the sensual heat from so long ago. His grey eyes were resting on her face, studying her every reaction.

"He can't save you."

Those cruel words came back with a vengeance. They were taunting her.

Townes wouldn't have told her that Moss was dead if he hadn't been given proof. Why, then, did she still feel his presence?

Shailyn involuntarily leaned into the man who made all her

fears disappear. She was well aware that others would say her attitude toward him made no sense considering he'd been a mere thirty-some feet away when Moss had initially taken her from the dance club. Even her own father had criticized Townes for his inability to stop Moss from abducting her in a public setting so easily.

What no one understood—or even listened to—was that she'd purposefully walked off by herself to spite Townes over something petty. She couldn't even recall what they'd been arguing about at the time.

"There's still a part of you that wants to touch the light." Townes wrapped his arms around her, despite the awkwardness of her helmet. She relished his warmth. "Please allow me to show you the way home, freckles. You've been gone for far too long."

Shailyn let herself have this moment a little bit longer. She'd changed her mind about keeping her distance from everything and everyone. She wasn't sure what the immediate future held, but she needed something to take with her when she left.

"Let's do this," Shailyn said softly, pulling away in determination. "I'm as ready as I'll ever be."

The smile on Townes' face said it all. She could count on one hand the times that she'd seen him beam in abject happiness. It simply wasn't in his nature. The wicked grin was so compelling that she lifted an arm and pressed her palm gently against his cheek to capture some of its essence.

Yes, she would take advantage of the time she had left with him before being sentenced to a life alone served in anonymity.

THE TINGLES OF *excitement ran up his spine at the broadcast being aired across all the national news channels.*

The confirmation of his death would allow him the ability to do so much more than squirrel away subsisting on memories as if he were still incarcerated in a federal prison.

Would Townes Calvert be gullible enough to swallow what was being fed to him?

Only time would tell.

And no one was more patient than the demon possessing his soul.

CHAPTER TWELVE

TOWNES LEANED INTO the sweeping curve in a manner as graceful as a lover's caress. The moment he righted the machine between his thighs and applied the throttle to pour on the speed, Shailyn's sweet laughter filled the air and eventually drifted away with the wind.

The cool air blew against his face and brought with it the enticing mix of scents from the dark night. The earthiness of the fields, the citrus honeyed fragrance of the grapefruits and orange groves, and even the dampness from the local canals made for a heady combination that smelled like freedom.

This was what they both needed after being on lockdown behind the fortress walls.

Townes was still somewhat uneasy. He'd given Shailyn the facts as they'd been reported to him, but every single nerve in his body was telling him that Moss was still alive. He was out there somewhere…waiting. He was anticipating the moment when he would strike to complete his masterpiece he'd only just begun, but that moment would never come if Townes was alive to prevent it.

An apex predator rarely surprised another. The closest comparison he could think of was an encounter between two lone male timber wolves circling an unclaimed female in the wild.

One wanted a mate, the other was sizing up a meal.

A decision needed to be made regarding Shailyn's long-term future, but he would see to it that it wasn't made tonight or tomorrow. The heat from the developing media storm needed to settle down, her parents had to be brought to the estate secretly and informed of the truth, and he wanted more time to prove that the DNA evidence uncovered at the cabin had been tampered with in some fashion. The latter would the most difficult of the three, but his team was currently hard at work to ferret out the break in custody or determine if there was another inside man on Moss' payroll.

Townes leaned his Harley into the next curve a little more than necessary, but he enjoyed the habit that Shailyn had of tightening her hold around his waist every time he shifted his weight. There was something so seductive in controlling a powerful machine and having a woman trust in his abilities to handle it, as well as being receptive enough to enjoy the freedom.

It was intoxicating as hell.

"Does this bike have another gear?"

Townes grinned at the enthusiasm in Shailyn's animated voice. She was having the time of her life, just as he'd hoped she would. He did her bidding and popped the bike up into sixth, piling on the gas. The motorcycle surged forward onto a straightaway, climbing past ninety and still accelerating fast. The trees alongside them were nothing but planks on a picket fence.

He'd had the additional security agents he'd posted around the property confirm that nothing and no one had been seen around the perimeter. There were even supplementary agents stationed along every likely avenue of approach looking for anyone who wasn't familiar or living in the immediate area.

This motorcycle ride wouldn't last for long, and he would

keep to those areas he'd specified to the added agents who had previously scoped out the preplanned route, however random it appeared to Shailyn. The outing would be just enough to give Shailyn what she needed before returning to the safety of the compound and its high-tech security perimeter.

Who was he kidding? This ride was meant to boost the mental health of both of them.

"You doing okay back there?" Townes called out when he felt Shailyn apply some pressure to her legs to slightly adjust her position behind him. The passenger on a bike could easily shift the center of gravity if they moved too much. Thankfully, Shailyn didn't possess enough weight to counter his bulk. What really concerned him was the fact that there had been some muscle damage as a result of the wounds she'd suffered from Moss. "Need a break?"

"No." Shailyn rested her upper body against his back to reaffirm her answer. "Keep going!"

Townes allowed them another half hour of freedom to enjoy the countryside. It was as if this were in their own private oasis. Not a single vehicle was seen on the road, not that they weren't being tracked. The only living presence had been in the golden eyes of the occasional little critter using the safety of the darkness to hunt for food next to the rural route.

Neither one of them could have asked for a more enjoyable ride.

"Take a moment to get your legs back under you," Townes directed tenderly, making sure that she could stand without assistance. He used his body to hold up his Harley while offering his hand to her. He hadn't missed the wince that crossed her features when she'd swung her leg over the back of the bike. "We were out for quite a while."

"I'm good." Shailyn's cheeks were flushed and a hint of that sparkle in her emerald green eyes had returned. "That was so exhilarating!"

"I'm sure we can carve out some time tomorrow to do it again if you want," Townes promised as he turned the key and allowed the engine to wind down. He removed his gloves and helmet before dismounting the bike, setting both items on the black leather seat. "Come here."

Shailyn had not made an attempt to take off her own helmet. He carefully unsnapped the button and pulled the strap through the metal ring, feeling the heat of her gaze resting on his face. His forced his concentration to the task at hand. Now wasn't the time to push his agenda or challenge any roadblocks.

Hell, he didn't like thinking of their future in those terms. They'd been separated for years, with good reason. He understood they needed time to get to know one another again, but as far as he was concerned, neither one of them would have to live their lives alone any longer. Whatever it took to see to it that they were given another chance…well, he would do what had to be done.

"We'll give the news time to settle over the public before I have your parents brought here to the estate." Townes carefully lifted the helmet over her head before setting it down on top of the padded sissy bar. Bringing up her reason for being here conveniently allowed her to put some space between them if she needed it. The overwhelming attraction between the two of them was becoming more and more intense the longer they were in each other's company. "In the meantime, I'm sure we can find some B-rated movie on the dish. I might even have some microwave popcorn."

"Townes?"

His name falling from her lips prevented him from taking a step forward. The frogs and crickets were still deep in conversation surrounding the estate, though some clouds had rolled in above and were currently hiding the moon. The dark of the shifting sky converged over them more and more, reminding him that they were far from clear of this investigation.

"You don't think he's dead, do you?"

Townes truly thought she was going to thank him for the ride, maybe even ask if he was willing to watch some chick flick on television. All her inquiry did was prove to him that neither one could shake the suspicion that this case was far from over.

"The DNA samples matched what was in the system." Townes purposefully took a step, and then another, until she had no choice but to fall in line beside him. He understood her need for reassurance, but he wasn't going to allow Moss to take away the sense of freedom she'd gained this evening. "Do you still like butter on your popcorn?"

"The more, the better," Shailyn quipped after a moment of silence. She wanted to press the issue, but she had thankfully taken his lead. "And salt. Lots and lots of popcorn salt."

Townes opened the door on the screened porch after surveying their surroundings. He was proud of what he'd accomplished here, and he wanted her to see the value of what her future could hold with the connections he'd made. He was making progress, but the real test would come when or if things regained status quo.

Did he believe Moss was dead? No, not at all. Townes wouldn't believe such a statement until he saw the corpse with his own eyes.

"Why don't you go find us a movie on television while I make the popcorn?" Townes removed his leather jacket and hung it from one of the hooks on the antique coat rack in the corner of the foyer. It was rare the vintage accessory was ever used, but he appreciated the history associated with the hand-carved wood. He helped her out of her coat, only to see her adjust the scarf tied securely around her neck. There would come a time when she didn't feel the need to shield him from her scars, but it wouldn't be tonight. "You'll find the remote on the coffee table. Hit the movies button and select menu."

It didn't take Townes long to microwave a bag of movie theater popcorn, sprinkling on additional Morton's popcorn salt. He grabbed two bottles of water and some napkins before carrying the large bowl into the living room. Shailyn was curled up underneath a blanket in the middle of the couch. Her eyes were glued to the numerous strands of Christmas lights adorning the large Leyland Cypress tree Brody and Remy had found on the south side of the property.

"You couldn't find a movie?" Townes asked as he set all the items next to the remote control on the coffee table. Some loose strands of his hair had come out of the tie he'd used to secure them at the base of his neck, so he reached behind him and took out the black band. "Not even an old Sly Stallone action flick?"

"I was thinking maybe you could get me caught up with your life since the trial," Shailyn prompted softly, leaning forward for the bowl of popcorn. She patted the brown leather cushion next to her and peered up at him through her lashes. He didn't like where this was going, but he came to terms with the fact that this was part of building what he hoped was a better future. "What did you do after he was convicted?"

Townes gave a resigned sigh as he settled in beside her, not bothering to reach for the remote. He ran a hand over his jawline, causing his fingertips to run across the scar. She wanted details of the years they'd been apart. He wasn't so sure where to start.

"I ran with the clubs for a while longer. One percenters mostly," Townes answered honestly, thinking back on that time with fondness. "I wasn't in a good place, and the members accepted my boundaries as a friend of the different clubs. I made connections, stayed in contact with several friends in and out of the service, and also began to integrate myself with the federal authorities on a couple different levels."

"You realize that those three things contradict one another, right?" Shailyn wasn't the type to toss numerous popcorn puffs into her mouth. She was way too graceful for that, and she would choose a specific popped kernel that contained more butter than the next to carry to her rosy lips. It was quite sensual in a manner she wasn't even aware of in her search for answers. "I mean, the one percenters aren't known to stay within the boundaries of the law by definition. How does one become a Special Chief Deputy U.S. Marshal while running with a crowd who technically doesn't follow the letter of the law?"

"It was a rather circuitous route," Townes replied with a slow smile. He wasn't a Boy Scout, but he did stand on the lighter side of the fight for right versus wrong. He sometimes took judicious shortcuts to meet his objectives. "Actually, it was a few years after that when I came to be employed by a special contractor running an agency based out of Minneapolis to oversee the protection detail of one of their employees. It was a favor for an old friend sort of thing, but let's just say the assignment involved the Defense Department in some form or fashion. One thing led to another. A job offer was made, I tried it, and then decided working for someone else in a structured environment wasn't in the cards for me. A silent partnership was formed so that SSI could come into existence. Certain allowances were made to establish federal jurisdiction not limited by regional offices and the Marshals Service was the best fit. I received my current appointment from the last Director of the USMS at the request of the Attorney General as directed by the

President."

"And the Special Chief Deputy U.S. Marshal's badge means you work for Uncle Sam?"

"Only since the day after Moss escaped federal prison. Prior to that, I was technically a private contractor with federal arrest powers."

Townes' time in Minneapolis had been a wakeup call that he was wasting his life and not living up to his potential. He'd become withdrawn and living on automatic, endlessly smoking cheap cigars by the box. Seeing what his dear friend had created for himself made Townes realize that all was not lost. All he had to do was take the bull by the horns and snap his damn neck. In this most recent case, his unique skillset was needed to take down a serial killer for the second time…permanently. That had been the consensus from the Florida DOC.

"SSI was meant to take government contracts the federal authorities didn't want or have time for while pursuing their very narrow focus to defeat terrorism inside the United States, her protectorates, and territories. That didn't go exactly as planned when one of the first cases we took on happened to be a stalker targeting a federal prosecutor. Though we did have a special insight on that case."

"Ashlyn." Shailyn had been here long enough to get to know everyone. Though this house happened to be gigantic by most people's standards, it was almost small enough to be considered cozy having twelve people under one roof. She hadn't been in most of the outbuildings or the guard shack, but she'd made a respectable attempt to meet everyone on the estate, including the sentries. That would change eventually, though, giving Townes the privacy he desired to be with Shailyn. "Cailyn and Remy were also targeted by a couple of twisted individuals, from what I've heard. I am sorry that Camryn got caught up with one of

Moss' sick devotees."

"You and I both know that's not even remotely your fault." Townes ran a hand through his hair as he shook his head in answer to her offer of popcorn. He was only hungry for one thing, but that wasn't currently on the menu. "Moss was targeting someone connected to me specifically. His attempt thankfully backfired at diverting my attention in any meaningful way. In fact, it focused all our efforts."

"What will you do now that Moss is out of the picture?" Shailyn had stopped eating the salty snack as she waited for his answer. "Has SSI gotten a reputation for handling those types of cases? Or will you try to redirect your business toward those government contracts you initially wanted?"

"I'm not sure where the future will lead us." Townes would make that decision when the time came. He tried not to let the double entendre land too heavy. He wasn't so sure they were done with the one investigation the public thought had been completed with a tight red bow. "The next few days will be about reconnecting you with your parents, going over your options, and seeing to it that whatever decision you make allows you the freedom to live your life without fear."

Shailyn didn't respond. He believed it was due to his evasive answer regarding Moss' demise. She switched topics, asking lighthearted questions about his travels across the country. She understood that he'd created a family of his own with SSI, so there was no need to mention his parents. They'd been out of the picture since before he entered the Marines. His mother by death, and his father by choice.

"I have something for you," Shailyn said softly, leaning forward so she could reach into the back pocket of her white jeans. To say he was surprised at what she held in her fingers was an understatement. "I thought maybe you'd want this back."

The Christmas lights on the tree glinted off the gold coin that he'd carried with him throughout his numerous deployments and even more bar fights. She held it gently in her fingers, as if the lucky charm held some kind of special magic.

Maybe it did.

They'd both survived impossibly life-threatening situations while it was in their possession. Maybe it was their lucky charm.

Townes had asked the prosecutor in Moss' trial to give Shailyn his coin, knowing she'd appreciate the gesture. It was his way of giving her a piece of himself without physically being by her side. She'd already heard his tale of how it was the only thing of value his mother had on her deathbed, though the monetary value wasn't the real reason he'd always carried it with him.

"Thank you for allowing me to borrow it." Shailyn would have pressed the coin into the palm of his hand had he not covered her fingers with his. "Townes, you can have it back."

"No," Townes replied, not willing to take back the only thing that connected them. "You keep this with you, freckles. I'll take it back when I'm one hundred percent sure that Moss and all of his crap are finally out of our lives for good."

CHAPTER THIRTEEN

S HAILYN WAS BACK to her regular sleeping habits of getting two hours here and there. It appeared that those four hours she'd managed to attain in Townes' arms the other night was a one-off. A part of her longed to see if it could happen again, but she didn't want to be the cause of his lack of rest. She was fairly sure he hadn't slept with her in his arms. He, too, was running on little sleep as it was.

The sun was slowly rising over the horizon, casting an orange glow over the peaceful water of what she would call a small lake. It certainly didn't look like a pond, the way Townes described it. She was standing on the deck overlooking the massive body of water on the estate's immediate northern side, contemplating the various avenues that were in front of her. Honestly, she couldn't remember a time she watched the sun rise without being behind a window. She was afraid she could get used to this.

One of the U.S. Marshals had mentioned during her ordeal that Moss' trial had received so much national press coverage, it was doubtful she could ever leave the witness protection program. The FBI once gave a public statistic of twenty to fifty active serial killers in the United States, and that didn't include the psychopaths who thought it might be fun to try and get their name in the paper by finishing what Moss started or his acolytes who followed him like a god.

Yet this sanctuary Townes had created here made her think such a thing as claiming back her life was eventually possible. In the days spent under his roof, she'd stopped checking her personal items to see if they'd been moved. She didn't feel the urge to examine every lock in the house to ensure they were secure. She could trust others to keep her safe.

The problem she encountered every time she thought about salvaging what was left of Shailyn Doyle was that every scenario involved keeping Townes in her life.

He had his own personal reasons for taking her out of WITSEC. Moss had become his adversary, and Townes needed to motivate his opponent.

Was she just a means to an end?

Shailyn had never once given thought to being with a man after the agony she suffered under Moss' hands. Her body was no longer something anyone would want to see, but for Moss or one of his minions. She bore so many scars on her flesh that it was near impossible to recall what she once looked like with fair, unblemished skin.

Was it possible to be loved for who she was on the inside, or was that just a fairytale to make damaged women feel better about themselves?

"Good morning."

Shailyn startled as she turned to find Brody walking up the wooden steps from the path that led to his open office next to the team room. He was wearing one of those bright, colorful Hawaiian shirts he had a penchant for, but it was the manila folder in his hand that caught her attention the most. She was curious as to the news it might hold. His ability to sneak up on her like that made her realize she was getting too complacent, even for the fortress that Townes had built.

"Good morning." Shailyn shook her right hand to try and ease the burning generated from the hot liquid that had sloshed over her fingers when she turned so suddenly. She was grateful when Brody stopped by the patio table where some napkins were positioned in an adorable square flower vase. She had a hard time believing Townes had chosen such décor, but he was constantly surprising her. Technically, everything that had happened over the last few days had astounded her. "Thank you."

Shailyn took the napkins and wrapped it around the white porcelain mug she'd brought outside. The coffee soaked into the white material, causing it to stick. It was better than nothing, and she wasn't ready to go back inside the house. She wanted to know what it was that he had discovered.

"You're up early." Brody's tone suggested he was aware of her secret in that she didn't sleep much, but he continued talking before she could address his assumption. "Is Townes in the kitchen yet?"

"No." Shailyn once more eyed the manila folder in his hand. A familiar unease settled over her at the thought that Brody had some news regarding Moss. "Did you find something that contradicts the DNA results?"

Brody appeared rather shocked by her question. He didn't miss a beat, though.

"No, not at all." He hesitated before joining her at the wooden railing. "You know, it would be an anomaly should the body turn out to be anyone other than Moss. DNA is ninety-nine percent accurate when sampled and processed by a certified lab, not to mention the FBI forensic guys."

"I was a victim of a serial killer," Shailyn reminded him wryly. It was easy to see that she'd made strides in accepting her past. Her therapist would be very proud she could talk about the former event without having an anxiety attack. She leaned her forearms against the wood and stared out over the calm water. Maybe this place was magic. "I was already in that one percent group when I survived an attack of that nature."

"I like you," Brody said with a smile as he crossed his arms and leaned back against the railing. "Look, we're going at this from every angle in the known universe. I understand that Moss' intelligence is off the charts. Is it a possibility he somehow paid off some technician to fuck with the results or the sample? Absolutely. Which is why we're doing deep background checks and interviews on anyone who was in the chain of custody of those DNA samples. Moss also had no siblings we are aware of, so a familial DNA match is out."

"Why would a sister or brother..." Shailyn let her words trail off as she finally comprehended his meaning. "You considered that maybe the body was that of a close relative."

"Like I said, we're not ruling anything out. Our job is to confirm even the slightest possibility that the corpse wasn't Moss."

"Brody." Both he and Shailyn turned at the sound of Townes' voice. She was used to him being serious, though he tended to be a little more lighthearted around her for obvious reasons. The man standing just outside the patio door wasn't someone she knew. "I'd like to speak with you in my office."

"Townes, he was just—"

"Now," Townes barked, causing his loose strands to fall and conceal half his face. "Shailyn, you have the day to relax. Your parents are scheduled to be here tomorrow at noon, so I'll have lunch served in."

And just like that, the patio door was void of his presence.

"I-I'm sorry," Shailyn said in somewhat disbelief. "He

shouldn't have—"

"His bark is much worse than his bite," Brody shrugged off, as if this part of Townes appeared more often than it should. "You need to remember something, Shailyn."

She forced herself to look away from the sliding glass doors. Brody didn't appear at all bothered with the way Townes had addressed him. In fact, there was a smile on his face as if he were a kid about to enter an arcade with a pocket full of quarters.

"Calvert has spent the last four months tracking Moss down. I'm not talking about eight-hour days, either. This entire team has lived and breathed this investigation, but not like him." Brody tapped the manila folder on his leg as if he were second guessing finishing his thought. "I didn't need special software or a fancy degree from MIT to connect the dots, Shailyn. Calvert didn't build this estate with all the state of the art security measures for SSI."

Brody's name resounded through the walls of the house, traveling out the open glass door. He only laughed and shook his head, turning on those leather flip-flops of his as he crossed the threshold.

He'd left her with some questions that only Townes could answer.

Why *had* he come back to Florida? He had no family here. He could have established SSI in Washington D.C. or some other major city in the U.S.

Was Brody suggesting it was because of her? If so, Townes was a Special Chief Deputy U.S. Marshal. He easily could have come for her at any time over the years. Yet he hadn't.

"When was the last time you had a mani-pedi?"

Shailyn was caught off guard once again by Camryn's sudden presence. The gorgeous actress was standing in the exact spot her brother had just vacated. Her natural beauty was rather intimidating in person.

"Um, I'm not sure I ever had one from a professional," Shailyn answered honestly, thinking back to the days when she lived a normal life. She then peered at the fingernails of her right hand and closed them tight into her palm. There really wasn't anything there to work with. "I don't think—"

"Oh, don't bail on me now," Camryn pleaded, closing the distance between them. She grabbed ahold of Shailyn's wrist and guided her toward the door. "I might not be as good as a professional in a nail salon, but I'm not too shabby. Ash had to go into the office, Cailyn is meeting some other reporter in town to work on an article, Remy went to work at the advertising agency, and Brett is on some conference call with the superintendent of her school and the school board. I need something to do. Besides, this will be fun. We can do some online Christmas shopping while we soak our feet. I've got a platinum card with no limit just waiting to be abused."

Camryn was a force to be reckoned with and it was obvious that Shailyn wasn't going to be able to say no. Maybe it wasn't such a bad idea, after all. She was seeing her parents for the first time in years. She would like to make a good impression, and that included them not concentrating on the few scars visible on the back of her hands. The majority were on her arms, legs, and torso. Still, she would feel better conveying an appealing facade.

Shailyn's acquiescence had nothing to do with the fact that they would be inside the house, close to Townes' office. She couldn't help but sigh in resignation upon finding his office door closed. Just what had been in that folder Brody had in his hand? Her curiosity was bound to get the best of her, but she would be patient.

After all, she'd waited this long for her life to change. What was a few more hours?

His face was still splashed across every news channel. It was rather satisfying to know he was of such importance in the public's eye. Unfortunately, it was only a matter of time before something remotely newsworthy happened that would replace him, like some moron dropping a krugerrand in the pail of some grocery store Santa.

It was then that he would set his plan in motion.

He pushed off the rotting planks of the wooden porch with his shoe to set his rocking chair in motion. He was but a half mile from where his death had taken place. There was something very satisfying about being so close to the very site of his supposed demise.

Was Calvert starting to believe he was free of their past?

It would only be then that the fun would truly begin.

CHAPTER FOURTEEN

"**Y**OU KNOW THAT Brody is going to grant himself a rather hefty bonus after this morning's briefing," Sawyer said without looking up from the scattered papers in front of him. He was sitting at the kitchen table, still going through the old case files of Caroline Marinovic. "Now might be a good time to hire some of that support staff you mentioned a few months ago."

Townes didn't take the bait. He was leaning against the counter, waiting for a fresh pot of coffee to brew. Wrong pot, right grounds was all he was thinking at the moment.

For some reason, today had been difficult. This waiting to see if Moss would make another move was more irritating than not knowing what the future held for him and Shailyn. One couldn't happen without the other, as if they were dominos about to fall.

Was Moss truly dead? Had he taken the coward's way out because he had some irrational belief that he could spend eternity with the women he'd killed? Was he so deluded in the end that he believed the afterlife for him was filled with his victims acting as his servants? Was it even possible that it could truly be over?

The vibration of his cell phone was a welcome relief. It also

spared him from having to answer Sawyer. He stood upright as
he answered the call, an old habit left over from his time in the
Corps.

"Calvert." He listened intently as Keane identified himself
and finally gave the team something to chew on. "Where has
Grove been all this time?"

Sawyer immediately started to gather the case files together
in anticipation of locking them up before leaving the compound.
Townes had to have missed something in the conversation.

"Wait," he ordered, even holding up his hand in a useless
gesture. "Repeat what you just said."

Townes quickly pulled the phone away from his ear and
pressed the speaker button so that he wouldn't have to reiterate
this new development to Sawyer.

"You heard me right the first time," Keane replied over the
open line with a hint of disbelief himself. "Grove is currently in
a Miami hospital recovering from overexposure and some
second-degree burns. It appears he went on a two-man alligator
hunt in the Everglades approximately two weeks ago. He didn't
think to tell his family, because it was planned as a one-day
excursion. Well, he and his tour guide were allegedly robbed at
gunpoint of all their belongings, including their boat. Then they
were subsequently abandoned in a rather remote area without
any survival gear."

Townes didn't for one second doubt that Moss had a hand
in arranging Grove's misfortune. Unfortunately, the man's bad
luck occurred around fourteen days ago…well before Shailyn's
death was reported in the media. Did this strange development
change the course of the investigation? Not in the slightest.

"Head down to Miami," Townes directed, knowing that
Keane was with Royce. "Interview both Grove and the tour
guide. Try and get a more complete picture of what took place

with possible descriptions of the culprits. While you're there, do a little digging into his fiancée's death. See if his story changes from his original account in any way."

"We'll be in touch."

Townes was now at the island facing Sawyer who stood on the other side. They both turned at the sound of the sliding glass door opening, revealing Brody. It was apparent by his expression that he had some news for them, causing Townes to think of the old adage—*when it rains, it pours.*

"The second sample of DNA we sent to DOJ for testing came back. It was in the ninety-third percentile as a match for Moss." Brody walked around the counter and over to the refrigerator. He pulled out a beer and popped the cap as he settled back against the fridge. "I'm inclined to say that Moss is in fact dead."

"Moss isn't dead." Townes was getting real tired of being the only one with certainty on this subject matter. "Run the DNA sample again."

Townes poured himself a cup of coffee and then left the room, leaving the men to discuss how he was most likely wasting resources. Well, they were his resources to waste, so let it be done.

He purposefully walked past the living room without a glance to where Shailyn was curled up on the couch and doing some online Christmas shopping for her parents. Christmas was mere days away and this would be the first time she'd be able to give a present to her parents in years. Camryn had strict instructions to use her own credit card so there wasn't a trace leading back to Shailyn.

He entered his office and quietly closed the door behind him.

Four hours later, Townes was still immersed in the Caroline

Marinovic files. It provided him with the distraction from Shailyn that he needed, especially considering he didn't want to push her into making a rash decision about her future without thinking things through. She needed to see for herself that this sanctuary he'd provided her could benefit the both of them, even if he wasn't within arm's reach.

It had also given him time to flesh out his white board project, pinpointing each and every milestone in Moss' life. If he were dead, this would all be a waste of time.

"You should be getting some sleep," Townes said from his position in his favorite chair. He'd been staring at the white board for the last thirty minutes, attempting to see the timeline from a different perspective when he'd caught the slight movement inside the doorway. "Tomorrow's a rather big day for you."

"I heard Brody talking to Remy about the new confirmation from another accredited government lab that the DOJ uses for high profile cases." Shailyn moved farther into the room. One arm was crossed around her waist. She used it as a prop for her other elbow, allowing her to appear in a somewhat natural pose with her other hand covering her neck. "I couldn't help but wonder if you now believe that it really was Moss in that cabin."

Townes wasn't about to take away her hope for a brighter future. Besides, he was too taken aback that she was wearing more casual clothes that didn't include a scarf. She had on a pair of joggers and a long-sleeved thin shirt that she clearly wore to sleep in.

"We located Caroline Marinovic's fiancé. Keane and Royce drove down to Miami to interview him." Townes unfolded his large frame from the chair, leaving the white board until tomorrow. The woman standing in front of him was more important. "Coen is leaving first thing in the morning to go back to the crime scene. Sometimes it's beneficial to look at things from a different angle after some time has gone by."

"I spent day after day, week after week, month after month, and year after year perfecting my patience as the seconds ticked by with only my computer to keep me company." Shailyn spread her fingers a little wider across her neck in response to his proximity. "These last few days feel like an eternity compared to those years. What are you…"

Shailyn would have stepped back at his attempt to lower her hand from her neck, but he'd wrapped his fingers around her wrist. He observed the flush from her cheeks fade and her perfectly shaped lips thin out as he revealed some of her scars. He didn't think about what he was about to do, nor did he consider the ramifications. Any fallout from his actions could be remedied. He refused to believe otherwise.

"Every one of these scars are a testament to your strength." Townes slowly leaned down and pressed his lips against the worst mark that he only saw as beautiful. Her entire body had gone still, and she'd stopped breathing. He kissed another. "I, for one, only see your beauty."

Townes tenderly kissed each blemish visible above her neck-line. There weren't many, but there were enough to make her self-conscious as hell. He would spend the rest of his life proving to her that she no longer needed to hide. His purpose had started the day he'd brought her here and wouldn't end until he could no longer draw air into his lungs.

A lone tear fell from her cheek.

Shailyn had shown no other outward sign that she'd given in to her sorrow. A piercing pain slashed through his heart at her stoic reaction to his affection. He wanted her to be able to derive as much strength from him as she needed, but she was still blind to what he'd spent so long building. She didn't know yet, nor recognize, that his admiration for her had turned into love long ago. She hadn't been here all this time to see the transformation.

Townes gathered her against him, grateful that she didn't push him away. He shifted so that he could lift her into his arms and carry her back to his chair. It hadn't been his intention to hold her so intimately, but the dam had broken. Shailyn cried for what had been and for what was left.

There was no need for words.

He simply held her while she released all the grief and anger that had been coiled inside of her for way too long. It wasn't until he sensed her muscles relaxing one by one that he allowed his own anguish to reveal itself. He cried with her. For just this moment in time, he allowed himself to purge the suffering he'd experienced over the years.

CHAPTER FIFTEEN

S HAILYN WOKE TO sunshine. She closed her eyes once more and laid there for a moment, mulling over in her mind what was wrong with this scenario.

Peace.

She was experiencing peace and what a wonderful sentiment it was in the bright morning light.

"Your coffee is on your side of the bed on the nightstand."

Shailyn slowly smiled at the rasp of Townes' voice and the way he referred to her *side of the bed.* Most men would wake up speaking in that rough manner, but it would fade by their second or third word. Not Townes. His vocal cords had been damaged in some way that he'd yet to share.

"I'm warm."

"The sun is shining directly on you, woman."

Leave it to Townes to point out the obvious. He understood exactly what she meant, but he wasn't allowing her to go there.

"I didn't dream about him, either."

Shailyn lifted her lashes, but Townes was nowhere in sight. She leaned up on her elbows to find that he was watching her from his position at the bottom of the bed. It was as if he were searching her expression for something only he would recognize. She broke eye contact to look around the room...his room.

"I might have slipped you a sleeping pill last night."

Shailyn quickly brought her gaze back to him to see if he were telling the truth, but his small grin gave him away.

"I wanted to be here when your parents arrived, but Coen's found something that I need to personally see for myself out at the site."

Townes wasn't dressed in his usual pair of faded jeans. In their place was a pair of black dress pants. It was then she realized that he held a tie in his hand. Something had happened. She sat straight up, her previous unusual warmth evaporating. She missed it already.

"Why?"

"I want you to focus on your parents today," Townes said, trying to divert her attention. It wasn't working, but he took her by surprise when he walked around the side of the bed and softly pressed his lips to her forehead. Visions of last night flooded her mind. "They may try to influence your decisions, freckles. Don't let the distractions pull your attention away from what is important."

Shailyn wasn't able to find her voice before Townes picked up his shoulder holster and left the bedroom. She sat there rather helplessly and tried to gather her thoughts. Last night had been unexpected. When was the last time she'd broken down like that? Granted, the intimate feel of his lips against her bare skin...against her scars...had almost broken her. It *had* broken her.

She lifted a hand to her neck, realizing that she hadn't covered the disfigurements during their conversation. Her life was changing rapidly, yet it wasn't permanent. Was she setting herself up for heartbreak once again? Was it possible this brief safety would be ripped out from under her before she was ready to say goodbye? Her father wasn't going to be part of that decision this

DEADLY PREMONITIONS   123

time.

"You've faced this before," Shailyn whispered to herself as she tossed the covers aside. She swung her legs over the side of the bed. His bed. She wanted it to be hers too. Butterflies invaded her stomach at having reached a decision, and they became even more agitated when the door reopened to reveal Townes. "I don't want to go back to WITSEC."

To say that he appeared taken aback by her abrupt declaration was an understatement. He'd evidently returned for his suit jacket that was lying over the end of the bed, but he made no move to retrieve it.

Had she made a mistake? Had she misread his intentions?

"I want more."

Townes had composed himself and slowly closed the distance between them. He knelt beside the bed in front of her, though they were still eye level given his large frame. He didn't touch her, but set both hands on either side of her. His grey eyes had darkened into what she could only describe as an oncoming storm.

"Do you only want this safety I'm giving you, or do you want everything that comes with it?"

Townes was asking if she wanted *him*.

"It's not this place that provides me shelter, Townes. It's *you*." Shailyn placed a tentative hand on his cheek. "You give me warmth. Your presence allows me to sleep. I'm at peace when I'm with you, which tells me that the connection we share can't be severed by distance or time. I don't want to be forced to walk away from you ever again."

Townes rested his large hand over hers, turning his head so that he could kiss her palm. Warmth flooded her, but this time it wasn't unexpected. Her soul mended a little more from his tender touch.

"Calvert, we need to—" Sawyer broke off his statement when he caught sight of them from the hallway. Townes must have left the door open when he came to retrieve his jacket, but she didn't mind being caught in such an intimate position. It had become clear from meeting the team in Maine that they understood the depth of their feelings for one another. "Sorry. I'll be waiting downstairs when you're ready."

Shailyn let her gaze drift back to Townes, who hadn't been fazed by the interruption in the least. He was so formidable in his wants and needs. His confidence in what *could be* led to her strength.

"There are still quite a lot of loose ends that I'd like to see dealt with before we make any decisions." Townes brought her hand down to her lap, but never released his grip on her fingers. Had she misread his signals? Her stomach knotted. She would have pulled away from his touch had he not stopped her. "Let me reword that, because it's clear you misunderstood me. I want you here, freckles. Too many years were spent apart, and I'm partly to blame for that. I allowed outside influences to sway my instinct of what was right. Be assured, that will never happen again. But I also understand the tremendous impressions you're experiencing from the possibility that Moss is dead."

Townes thought she was reacting on emotion. He wasn't wrong, but he was incorrect about his belief that she might be confusing her reasons for wanting to here...for wanting him.

"Let me be clear." Shailyn couldn't prevent the catch in her breath at the intensity of his gaze. "I want you here. But should you decide to stay, that's it. I won't let you go for any reason under the sun, and I'll fight anything or anyone who tries to stand in our way—including your father or even your own fear. We will live in every way as a normal, loving couple."

Shailyn managed to swallow the lump in her throat after

Townes spelled out for her the meaning of this firm stance. Her father was a very powerful man in his own right, and he did have a lot of sway with a good amount of influential people. As for the other implication, that remained to be seen. He hadn't seen her body in a very long time.

"Your parents are coming here to visit you. They still believe you're dead, and that is for a very valid reason, as you well know. I wish I could be here to stem the shock they're going to suffer, as well as buffer you from their anger toward my decision to hide that fact from them." Townes lifted both of her hands and pressed his warm lips against her knuckles. "I'll do my best to make it back before they leave this evening. I'm sure your father will have a few choice words dreamed up for me. Until then, enjoy this time with them. Deflect blame on me, if need be. You deserve some quality time with them, freckles."

And just like that, Townes left the room as if he'd never been back. He snagged his suit jacket with a long reach of his arm before he crossed the threshold. Did he know he'd left her breathless? Did he comprehend her body's response to his declaration regarding her decision? He basically claimed her as his own, and while that would have offended her had he said it in any other manner…his virility was intoxicating regardless of her fears.

Shailyn figured she stayed where she was in his room for at least another ten minutes before she composed herself enough to transit back to her own. It took her another hour before she was showered and dressed, though she'd gone through three outfits with six different scarves before deciding on the appropriate apparel. Most of her clothes were for lounging around the house. Her only saving grace was that she'd had to pack everything she owned, which included the eight or so ensembles she could wear in public when the rare opportunity arose.

"Knock, knock," Remy called out lightly with a rap on the door. Shailyn turned to see both the pretty blonde and Camryn standing in the hallway. Neither one of them would ever know the painstaking care she had to take when making herself presentable. It was hard not to experience a bit of envy. "Brody called up from his office. Your parents are five minutes out."

Shailyn nodded her appreciation for the early notification before turning to look at herself in the full-length mirror. She was back in her room and wishing Townes had been able to stay for this long overdue reunion. She wasn't ready to do this by herself. She needed his strength.

"You look beautiful. I love the navy blue scarf." Camryn had come to stand behind her, reaching around for the brush still in her grip. She met Shailyn's gaze in the mirror as she held up the brush for permission. "May I?"

"Of course," Shailyn replied, watching as the bristles drew back her auburn hair. Camryn did the same on the other side, combining the two sections together and twisting them in a beautiful knot. She held it in place and then peeked over Shailyn's shoulder for approval. "I love it."

"Here, use my clip," Remy offered as she let her blonde hair fall around her shoulders. "And look, your nails match your lipstick. I love it!"

Shailyn hadn't noticed it before, but the rose-colored polish did match her lipstick. She looked over her appearance one more time with satisfaction. Remy and Camryn's presence also helped in giving her the confidence she needed for the emotional reunion about to take place.

"Thank you." Shailyn had to clear her throat, but she managed to convey her appreciation for their friendship. She missed having this type of encouragement. "I think I'm ready."

"Need some backup? I've taken a course in self-defense

when it comes to overbearing parents."

Shailyn smiled when she saw Brett enter the room. Carter and Pam Doyle would no doubt remember the sweet little brunette from middle school. Should a distraction be needed, Brett would certainly be able to provide it.

"I would love some," Shailyn responded before taking a very deep breath to calm her nerves. She'd taken extra time with her makeup, but she highly doubted she would have any mascara left within the first five minutes of seeing her parents. She'd missed them so much. "I think I'm ready."

"Let's do this. We're right behind you."

Brett held out her hand, which Shailyn took gratefully. It wasn't long before all four women descended the staircase, where Ashlyn already had her hand on the doorknob of the front door.

A light buzzing sound took up residence in Shailyn's ears that eventually drowned out whatever was being said around her. Her vision had slightly tunneled to where all her concentration was on the entrance Ashlyn had revealed by opening the front door.

There stood her parents who were expecting to see Townes Calvert. No doubt they thought Townes had requested their presence to go over the details of Moss' death.

They'd both aged far more than Shailyn would have thought they would. Her mother was still a beautiful woman, but the grief of losing a child had taken its toll. Her pallor was visible against the black blouse she was wearing, as well as the slight puffiness around her green eyes. She stared at Shailyn in horror for a few moments before accepting that the person standing before her was truly her daughter and not some apparition sent to cause her more grief.

"My baby," Pam whispered in a strangled tone as she rushed

into the house and wrapped Shailyn in a protective embrace.

It had been so long since Shailyn had seen her parents, let alone been held by her mother. She clung to what had been and what could be. Tears for time lost, memories remembered, and the chance for a future fell from both their eyes.

She wasn't sure how long they stood in each other's arms, but eventually her father joined them. He embraced them both without a word, though he silently cried as he rested his forehead against her shoulder.

Her parents deserved an explanation, but now was the time for all of them to appreciate this moment…to recognize the value of family.

HE SIPPED THE *bitter coffee as he took in the cooler morning temperatures. He preferred tea, but this hot beverage would have to do.*

The cabin had been rather chilly last night. He hadn't lit a fire for fear it would draw attention from some random hiker or some idiot out to retrieve a souvenir from his nearby gravesite. It wouldn't do to have carefully arranged such a well thought-out plan, only to have it fail due to such a chance encounter with a well-meaning simpleton.

He would have taken a seat to enjoy the sweet melody from the birds had he not noticed the silence.

Why?

An unfamiliar discomfort settled over him at the unnerving stillness of the woods.

Something wasn't right.

Someone was coming to see him.

CHAPTER SIXTEEN

TOWNES STOOD BENEATH a very large oak tree draped in Spanish moss. He was grateful that he'd left his suit jacket and tie in the car. Though the air was relatively cool, what he was about to do wasn't conducive to the constraint of expensive fabrics.

"Did you get anything important from the sheriff?"

"No." Townes began to slowly roll up his sleeves as he studied the thick branches that led to his destination. "But we'll eventually need to notify him that forensics will be returning to the crime scene. I just want to buy us some more time before a ton of traffic disturbs the locals."

"I take it we're holding off for an hour or so then?" Coen waited until Townes was ready to proceed before handing over a pair of latex gloves. He didn't want to contaminate the crime scene this far into the game. "Moss could very well be alive and somewhere in this area."

"Yes, it wouldn't surprise me."

Townes had met with the local police, asking for a briefing on crimes in the surrounding areas, such as break-ins, missing persons, and small thefts. Should Moss have attempted to falsify his death, he would have wanted to keep his profile rather low. He would have stayed somewhere nearby within the surrounding area before attempting to find a way out after tripping the switch and lying low.

The wooden structure nestled in the heart of the tree all but proved that scenario, though it still wasn't enough evidence by the standard of the law.

"I'm impressed, Flynn." Townes decided the easiest path to take up to the camouflaged timber-built shelter was to the left of the tree. "This is easily a hundred and fifty feet out from the cabin with an elevated but clear line of sight."

"Something wasn't sitting right in the satellite imagery." Coen and Townes both looked back to where Sawyer was carefully surveying the hard ground. It would be almost impossible for anyone with tracking skills to get a good bead on Moss with this terrain. "I realized that the avenue of escape was slightly hidden from view by that lone branch off the smaller oak. Granted, it could easily have been nothing, but we were at a dead end."

"Well, it panned out."

Townes reached out and grabbed a hold of the closest branch, hoisting himself up until he was able to use another limb for leverage. Should this be how Moss escaped without anyone the wiser, it still didn't explain the body. How had Moss gotten his DNA to match?

"Call one of the better local outfitters and have them bring their bloodhounds out. The dogs should be able to pick up a scent if we can find something inside this structure. They can track scents in the air as well as on the ground. They are persistent as hell."

Townes finally reached the entrance to the rather small enclosure, which was large enough to accommodate a single man in comfort. A quick glance showed nothing of interest besides a few rotting boards here and there. He didn't take anything for granted. He positioned himself so that he could survey the inside in its entirety.

"Anything?" Sawyer called up, having made his way across the hundred and fifty yards from the cabin.

"No."

Townes took a moment, blocking out the sights and sounds of the surrounding forest. The clearing wasn't too large. Nature's reverberations were relatively constant. He needed to visualize what may have happened, though it sickened his stomach to think that Moss had been mere yards away watching as firemen scrambled to put out the fire and local law enforcement debated whether or not he was still inside.

It was then that he spotted the lone white bottle cap tilted sideways against one of the boards that appeared to be cracked where an old nail had been driven through the wood. There was no mistaking that it had been left here recently due to the brightness of the cap and lack of dust.

"Dale Kitner can be here in under an hour." Coen was referring to the individual who owned one of the best-known tracking dogs in the county. "I'm not so sure we'll be able to withhold this from the sheriff's department for much longer, though. Dale was having lunch with one of his deputies when I called."

"Reach out to the sheriff, then. Let him know to limit traffic in and out of the surrounding area so that we don't tip off Moss should he still be laying up somewhere in the area. I want roadblocks on every road, trail, and two-track leading into these woods. I also want them at least twenty miles outside of the immediate area." Townes carefully lifted the bottle cap, ensuring the latex glove he was wearing hadn't torn on the branches he'd used as leverage. He then turned the glove inside out to contain the evidence. "Also, get Dale back on the line. Tell him we may need to rip a few boards off here to give the hounds a scent to track. Ask him what the best scenario is for this type of search. Give him anything he needs."

Townes gave the inside of the lumbered shelter another quick onceover. He then carefully descended and handed off the latex glove with the cap inside to Sawyer. He let the two of them deal with phone calls to forensics, the feds, the sheriff, and anyone else who needed brought into this part of the investigation.

He surveyed the area as he walked back to his vehicle, wondering how long Moss had stayed up in that ragged structure. Had he waited for the exact moment when the authorities had cleared out? Or had he waited even longer, ensuring that no one would suspect he'd had a way off the property without being noticed?

Townes opened the driver's side door and reached inside for the folder containing the current satellite images Brody had printed off just this morning. He walked around the car and used the trunk as a temporary desk. He spread the numerous images across the heated metal, positioning the photographs as if he were looking down at the area.

The team had personally visited each and every cabin within a two-mile radius, but that search had taken place the night of the fire. Moss would have been snug up in that treehouse of his, no one the wiser with him that far up in the foliage.

Townes slid the red marker he'd attached to the manila folder off the front cover. He went through each cabin, circling the ones that were currently sitting empty. They would all need to be checked, but the ones he'd marked with an X could be done by the sheriff. It would give the man something to do, thus keeping him out of SSI's way while he shot the shit with his hunting buddies and local constituents.

"There's a chance Moss could be long gone," Sawyer point-ed out, most likely trying to curb expectations. He had a point. Plus, he was still holding the evidence that could prove Moss was in that wooden structure. Any good defense attorney could argue that the cap had been left behind before the fire. Townes would verify otherwise by tracking down the son of a bitch. "I'm not so sure we should put out an APB. An All-Points Bulletin would only give Moss the upper hand."

"Which is why you're going to head into town while Coen stays here to deal with forensics. I want you to hold the sheriff's hand and make sure word doesn't spread to anyone who doesn't need to know, especially from that loudmouth deputy that was with Dale."

Townes pulled his phone off its holder attached to his belt. Swiping the display alerted him to the time. Shailyn's parents should have arrived at the estate by now. He'd purposefully shoved any thoughts of her aside. Her sweet declaration that she wanted to stay had hit him hard in the chest. He hadn't expected to hear those words so soon, and he'd even gone the extra mile in giving her a warning to think over her answer.

He wasn't playing this time around. Should she decide to stay, there was no turning back. He accepted his many faults, one of them being that he was selfish. She was his, as far as he was concerned.

"Calvert, Keane and Royce are pulling into town now." Coen held his phone at an angle, clearly not wanting to yell into the receiver. "Do you want them to stay there or meet you at a rendezvous point?"

Time was of the essence.

"Change of plans." Townes gathered up the papers and shoved them inside the folder, along with the red marker. "Coen, don't leave this property until forensics is through with it. Help Dale with anything he needs. Have Keane and Royce take care of the sheriff and his troop of Barney Fife deputies. Sawyer, you're with me."

Townes opened the back door of his car and set the manila folder on the back seat. He was settled behind the steering wheel and waiting for Sawyer to hand off the evidence to Coen right when his phone rang. It was the number that belonged to the cell Brody had given Shailyn to use for emergencies.

"Are you okay?" Townes pressed the ignition button and waited for Sawyer to close the passenger side door before he slipped the gear into drive. He'd answered before his Bluetooth had kicked in, so he was able to take this call in private. "Did your parents arrive safely?"

"Yes, they're here," Shailyn answered softly, her heartfelt tone telling him that the reunion had been an emotional one. "They want to tell the family that I'm alive."

"Absolutely not." Townes wasn't going to debate this and would have Brody handle the problem should the need arise. He was hoping it wouldn't come to that. "Shailyn, we found something that might prove Moss isn't dead. I'm going to need your parents to stay there for the time being. You're going to need to convince them that your death needs to remain intact as public knowledge for the foreseeable future."

He never should have allowed her parents to visit the estate, at least not yet. Not once in this investigation had he believed Moss was dead. He had allowed forensic evidence to dictate his actions, and now they all might very well pay the price for that lapse in judgement.

"I'll take care of it." The disappointment in Shailyn's voice would have brought him to his knees had he not already been sitting. He gripped the steering wheel with his left hand to prevent himself from making her a promise he couldn't keep.

"Townes?"

"Yeah, freckles?"

He wouldn't put distance between them now when what she needed was his strength.

"Please be careful."

"I always am."

Townes disconnected the line and then clipped his phone back into the small case attached to his belt. He drove down the lane and then made a right, following a narrow two-track road that had seen better days. It didn't take long to reach the next unimproved gravel lane he believed would lead him straight to Moss.

"I texted Brody so that he was aware that Shailyn's parents might present a problem. He'll put the estate on lockdown."

Townes didn't doubt that was what Sawyer had been doing on his phone, but he couldn't worry about that now. He slowly drove the car as close as he could to the isolated cabin via a mental estimate on how long the lane was per the image. The side of the road was overgrown with weeds and wild branches hanging down from the trees overhead. It was all but impossible to pull the vehicle off the gravel path, so he stopped the car in the middle of the lane and shifted the gear into park.

"We're walking in from here."

Townes turned off the engine and reached for his weapon. He had never fastened his seatbelt, so he was able to draw his firearm from his shoulder holster with ease. It would have been nice to have a couple long guns, but they weren't outfitted for this type of hunt.

Sawyer remained silent as he opened the passenger side door with utmost care. They both automatically fell into a staggered line thirty feet from each other. Townes took lead while Sawyer was to his right and ten steps back.

With each stride, their senses heightened. Townes didn't doubt that Sawyer was experiencing the same déjà vu. It happened to every individual who had ever served in the military. These kinds of skills were never forgotten, though this type of career kept them sharper than most. Hand and arm signals were to be used from here on out.

Wildlife was rampant in these parts. This was Florida, after all. Mother Nature appeared to have sent her critters a little warning about a standoff that could possibly be taking place. The only sound he could currently make out was the low drone of the mosquitoes. Those suckers were an equal opportunity hunter. He didn't bother to swat them away. All his attention was on his surroundings and the remote cabin that was finally coming into view.

Townes motioned with his hand that he had the left side of the cabin covered. According to the initial reports, this was a hunter's retreat and currently unoccupied. There had been no signs of anyone inside, and that hadn't changed from the outside appearance. It wasn't until he reached the side of the porch that he caught sight of a coffee cup set down on the wooden porch beside a matching rocking chair.

Sawyer gestured he would remain in position on the right-hand side of the cabin where he had a visual of both the side and front. Townes continued to cautiously make his way around back to an overgrown field, noting nothing amiss. He didn't lower his weapon as he continued forward until he could motion for Sawyer to make their existence known.

"SSI," Sawyer called out loud enough so that there was no mistaking who they were. "We've got you surrounded. Come out with your hands in the air."

Adrenaline was pumping through Townes' veins at a NAS-CAR rate of speed, but one would never know it by the steady manner in which he held his weapon. Should Moss or anyone else attempt to come out the back, Townes would be ready.

He sure as hell didn't expect his cell phone to vibrate on his hip. He ignored the call, concentrating on the task at hand. Whoever it was would leave a message.

Sawyer took a step forward and yelled out instructions once more. No one heeded the warning, so he finally closed the distance until he disappeared from Townes' line of sight. It was clear he was going to attempt entry.

Townes suppressed his surprise upon hearing the lightest ricochet of a dog barking off the trees in the distance. They were quite a way from the crime scene, but the forest must be laid out in such a way that the trees carried the sound.

Son of a bitch. Moss may have heard them coming.

He remained in place, regardless that his gut was telling him Moss was long gone. It would explain the coffee cup left on the front porch. He had somehow sensed or heard something that alerted him to the fact that there were people back at the crime scene. Hell, maybe it had simply been the echo of a car door slamming.

Either way, Moss would be close by to see if the unexpected guests were reexamining the site or if the wooden structure in the old oak tree had been discovered.

Sawyer finally made an appearance, shaking his head that there was no one to be found. Townes reluctantly lowered his firearm, swearing under his breath.

Damn it.

His phone vibrated once more. Snatching it out of its holder, he glanced at the display.

Unknown caller.

Sawyer must have sensed the tension that came over Townes. He immediately started to scan the dense wooded area, bringing his weapon up at the ready.

"You're no fun, Calvert."

Townes had brought his phone to his ear without making a sound. He was already aware of who was on the other end of the line, so there was no need to greet him like an old friend.

"I'm sorry to ruin your idea of entertainment, Moss." Townes holstered his weapon, turning to face the one direction he would have taken had he been the fugitive. "Did you really think I would fall for something so obvious?"

"You must have thought the same of me."

"Shailyn died as a result of your handiwork." Townes wasn't about to let the cat out of the bag now. "I don't have to convince you of anything. I don't have the ability to change the past."

The long, drawn-out pause on the other end of the line let Townes know that Moss now wasn't so sure in his original assumption.

"You're lying." There was a mocking *tsk* coming through the receiver loud and clear. It came too late, though. Townes definitely had a hook embedded and it was only a matter of time before he could yank the line. A piercing shot of satisfaction hit home. "I want her back, Calvert. It's only a matter of time before I find her."

"We can stand here and debate all day long, but the fact is I'm wasting manpower and resources trying to bring you in while you hunt for nothing but a ghost. Caroline is just as dead, Moss, just like Shailyn. Neither are coming back, and you certainly wouldn't be wasting your time talking to me if you had proof otherwise." Townes paused for effect. "Did you see the pictures of her corpse? Did you tug on your pathetic dick when you saw those pictures, you sadistic, perverted, cold-packing coward? Her loss is the reason I get up every morning now, but

I'm guessing it's also the reason you're second-guessing yourself right now."

Another seed planted. Pretty soon, a garden full of weeds would lead Moss directly to the place where Townes needed him to go to end this charade once and for all.

"I've said it before, Moss." Townes met Sawyer's gaze, who nodded his approval on how this phone conversation was playing out. He'd deliver his final message and then disconnect the line. There was something to be said for having the upper hand. "I'll be seeing you real soon. I hope you're ready to die."

CHAPTER SEVENTEEN

S HAILYN STOOD BY the Christmas tree looking out over the front driveway, but there was no warmth to be had from the newfangled colored LED lights. The scent of the Leyland Cypress was heavy in the air. She wrapped her arms around her waist to capture what heat she could from her body. It was slight without Townes' embrace.

It struck her as odd after glancing back into the room that if Christmas morning was to come and all of them were still here, the space was large enough to accommodate the entire house. Yet, somehow, it had been arranged to make even a single couple feel cozy.

"You should get some sleep."

She would have laughed at Brody's statement had he not sounded so sincere. He'd been a tremendous help today in convincing her parents to carry on this ruse of her death. His insistence on the overwhelming level of danger was the turning point for her father. Honestly, it didn't take much convincing on Shailyn and her mother's part once Townes had called to let her know that Moss had blown his ploy of enticing her out into the open. Apparently, the men had just missed the fugitive on the front porch of a neighboring cabin in the rural southern Florida county.

The notorious serial killer was alive and well, itching for revenge.

The media had been notified, law enforcement officers on every level had been informed, and now a renewed manhunt was underway.

Would it ever end?

"I think I'll stay up and wait for Townes."

Brody's audible sigh let her know that he'd settled on the couch behind her. It wouldn't surprise her if he fell asleep waiting for her, considering he was running on as little sleep as she was over the course of this past week. At least she hadn't been staring endlessly at numerous computer screens for countless hours. He was lucky he could still focus his vision.

"Moss is making mistakes." Shailyn couldn't make out Brody's reflection in the window, because the living room lights behind her were still off. She'd been tempted to turn them on, but she hadn't wanted anyone to know she was downstairs. Brody must have noted the inside switch activation of the great room window security shutter and had come to investigate why it was open. She had turned on the Christmas tree lights just because she couldn't stand the darkness. "It's only a matter of time before we close the net around him."

"I don't mean to burst your bubble, but that very sentence has been said many times." Shailyn honestly didn't want to talk about Shepherd Moss. It was pretty much what she'd spent most of the afternoon discussing with her parents. She couldn't escape his legacy. It was starting to suffocate her like a wet blanket. "I appreciate how you handled my parents this afternoon, especially my father."

"They love you. I didn't think it would take much convincing to keep them on board once we heard the news of Moss' revival." The couch cushions rustled a bit as Brody became more comfortable. "Hey, do you know if that box next to your feet contains one of the new Tommy Bahama Hawaiian shirts? I saw my name on it earlier."

Shailyn bit back her smile, which was exactly what he was trying to coax her to do. Remy had purposefully wrapped the box with thin wrapping paper so that a specific logo could be seen, but she used the box for something else entirely. It was so secret that she hadn't even shared the contents with the rest of the group.

"I honestly don't know." Shailyn figured there was nothing she could say that would cause Brody to leave her by herself, so she continued this line of discussion. It was easier than talking about what the next few weeks could possibly entail. "Did you know that the other day was the first time I've taken the time to Christmas shop since I went into WITSEC?"

"Really?" Brody exclaimed as his excitement shined through. "I wear a large, if I'm on your list."

Shailyn laughed, giving the man what he wanted. He was relentless, but she could see why he would need to be in order to provide balance to this team of men. They each had their own quirks, but Townes had built himself a rough group who had melded into a family with the addition of their women. Just for a moment, she pictured herself as Townes' woman in their dynamic and it caused her to briefly smile again. She'd acknowledged their family interactions before, but it was amazing to see how each one of them supported the other, as if by painstaking design.

She inhaled deeply before finally turning on the fuzzy socks she'd put on earlier. She was still having trouble wearing shoes for any length of time.

Shailyn resigned herself to the fact that Brody wasn't going anywhere. One of the light switch panels was on the other side of the Christmas tree. She flipped several switches looking for the right combination and bathed the room in a golden hue.

"How much longer?" Shailyn rose an eyebrow when he pretended not to understand what she meant. She spelled it out for him after nodding toward the phone in his hand. "Don't tell me you don't know their exact location and their immediate plans. You probably created some app that tracks their every movement in real time and displays it on your phone."

"Oh, those programs already exist. People use them to keep track of their children." Brody brushed her assumption aside with the flip of his hand. "I had to get a little creative because of our business, but don't let my secret out of the bag. My platform just applies that same type of data by networking a set of extended range RFID chips to an overlay of the satellite map from Google Earth. It's just an additional way to track their movements should one or two of the team ever get into a situation where they don't have their phones. As long as a single member has comms, I can locate any specific team member within a quarter mile of that source with a microburst transmission from the individual tags every ten seconds. The software was uploaded to the team's phones, so we all have access. They automatically cross-communicate to update the network."

Brody had lost Shailyn the moment he'd started talking about RFID chips, but she nodded her head in understanding anyway. He was rather animated when describing what he created. She didn't want him to believe she wasn't interested in how he'd gone about creating such a program.

"The network is linked to our satellite service provider so that we always have comms and encrypted location services even when the team is in the boonies like they are now with no regular cell service. We can even piggyback our proprietary signal off another service's phone without the owner ever knowing their device is communicating with a tower."

Did Brody really think she understood a word he was saying?

"As long as their phone is turned on, the handshake protocol will retransmit our location data package as embedded pseudo random noise during their service's normal linkup to the tower. I injected the program into each of the cell provider's networks as a Trojan-type virus to look at their header information for our data package. They just forward it over the established phone lines during normal operations without know it."

Shailyn stared at Brody and realized he truly had no idea that she hadn't understood a word he said. She'd heard Keane mumble a time or two that Brody needed to speak in English and not tech, but this proved it. It was then that something occurred to her.

"Oh, my god. Don't tell me each of you had microchips planted inside of your heads." Shailyn was all for the safety of the team, but those extreme lengths went beyond the pale. She curled up in the overstuffed chair, adjusting her scarf so that the knot stayed to the side. "I can't picture Townes going for something that intrusive."

"Well, not microchips like you're thinking and certainly not in our heads, but something close to that. And trust me, it took a lot of convincing on my part. The entire system is very secure and has anti-hack protocols I designed myself."

Shailyn didn't miss the concerned glance Brody shot toward the staircase. This had something to do with either Remy or his sister.

"After Camryn was taken, it became rather clear that we're not the only ones who can become targets…especially in our line of work." Brody shrugged in response, allowing her to see that he wasn't concerned by the lengths needed to keep those he loved safe. "With everyone's knowledge and consent, we put a small ER-RFID tracer—about the size of a grain of rice—in the men's arms. Nine times out of ten, an agent will be told to lay down his phone, but they wouldn't even pick up the burst transmission from the tracer. It only lasts 7.8125 milliseconds."

"And the women?"

"Each woman chose a piece of jewelry she always wears against their skin. Their body heat provides the power to the tracer inside." Brody stretched his legs out in front of him, though he made no attempt to lay down. That meant that Townes was close to the house and would be arriving soon. "I have extras available."

Shailyn laughed once more, understanding that he was offering to put a tracker on a personal item or even provide the injection so that she could be located easily should the need arise. Had this been ten years prior, she would have told him he was insane for thinking that she would go for something like that. She understood the need for privacy more than most. With that said, she would have given anything to have had something so miniscule placed on an earring or bracelet that would have enabled the police to find her in that abandoned warehouse.

"Here." Shailyn took off the only piece of jewelry she wore daily on her right hand. It was a ring her mother had given her that had been passed down through the generations. At this point in her life, it was somewhat comforting to know someone was looking out for her wellbeing. If she ever changed her mind, she would just remove the transmitter. "Will this work?"

"Yes," Brody answered, leaning forward and taking the ring from her to study the design. He flashed one of his smiles as he turned it over, looking at the inside of the band. "I'll have it back to you first thing in the morning, freshly cleaned and activated."

"If this were under any other circumstances, I wouldn't agree to anything so extreme." Two beams of light entered through the window and slowly traveled across the far wall. A rush of relief washed over her. "Thank you, Brody."

"Anytime. You're family."

The way Brody answered let her know that he understood what she was acknowledging. There hadn't been a need for him to keep her company, but he'd done so anyway. She was surprised that he quietly left the room and ascended the stairs. He most likely had already spoken to Townes over the phone, but a lot had happened that changed the immediate future for all of them.

The house was so solid and the windows so thick that she barely heard the muffled sound of doors closing on the vehicles outside. It wasn't long before the front door opened and she was stepping into Townes' warm embrace.

She'd missed the heat of his body, the intimacy his words conveyed, and the shelter he provided. In the span of less than a week, he'd become a part of her physical makeup. How had she lived so many years in isolation? How had she been able to walk away from life for so long? Necessity was the mother of invention.

"It'll be okay, freckles," Townes murmured against her hair, tightening his hold around her shoulders. "The more time that passes, the better the likelihood Moss will believe you're gone."

"I've never felt so alive, though."

A discreet cough came from behind them. Sawyer had closed the door and set the alarm, patiently waiting for them to move out of the foyer.

"Where are Keane and Royce?" Shailyn asked with concern, reluctantly stepping away and giving both of them room to move farther into the house. "Has something else happened?"

"They're hanging back and overseeing the ground search for Moss. We didn't want to leave it to Barney Fife, Goober, and his cousins." Townes maintained a hold on his suit jacket before addressing Sawyer. "Get some sleep. We have an early day tomorrow."

Sawyer said his goodnights, but walked down the hallway and into the kitchen instead of climbing the stairs. Light bathed the hallway before the sound of the refrigerator door being opened traveled through the archway.

"Did you not eat on the way home?" Shailyn was used to not having an appetite, but she doubted that Townes had that problem. "You should get something to eat, as well. I should probably head upstairs to my room."

Townes regarded her quietly, causing her to shift uncomfortably. Had something else happened that he was afraid to tell her?

"Did seeing your parents change your mind?"

"Change my mind about what?" Shailyn was a little lost as to where he was taking this conversation. A cold shiver washed over her. "Are you talking about this morning? I honestly didn't bring up what the future may hold for me with them. They didn't ask, and I didn't feel the need to consult with them on that subject. We spent the afternoon getting caught up on what has happened over the past few years."

"I find it hard to believe that your father didn't want to say a few choice words to me."

"Why would you think that?" Shailyn said with a small smile. She then addressed what was on both of their minds. "And no, I haven't changed my mind about us. I want to stay here with you, even should Moss never be captured or killed. I understand why things were done the way they were during the trial, and I also accept my part in the aftermath. This isn't then, and circumstances have changed considerably. We're both older, we're wiser, and we're more circumspect than we were back then."

"Yes," Townes confirmed with confidence, even though his

day had been wrought with transgressions. "We are all of those things and more."

The darkening of his grey eyes had those previous butterflies returning to her stomach. He hadn't even so much as kissed her...truly kissed her the way he used to when they'd been together. She wasn't even completely sure that he wanted to be intimate in the way a normal relationship would be. The thing of it was, he didn't have to touch her to obtain a response. It was automatic. It was natural.

He shifted his jacket into his left hand and then held out the other for her to take. She didn't hesitate. She slipped her fingers into his and allowed him to guide her up the stairs, through the hallway and past the other bedrooms until they reached the second to the last door.

Shailyn understood why he stopped and waited, and recognized that this level of familiarity went beyond anything they had ever shared. She left him standing on the threshold while she gathered the few items she'd removed from her suitcase. It was now time to finally unpack her simple collection of belongings someplace other than a temporary home.

Townes startled her when his hand covered hers, taking the lone piece of luggage from her grasp. She picked up her tote and slid the straps over her shoulder, quietly following him into their room. He lifted the suitcase and set it on the bed facing outward so that she could easily access what she needed before he silently walked into the bathroom and closed the door.

Had he given her some privacy to get used to the idea of living and sleeping by his side? Technically, she'd done that a couple times since her arrival. This was different, though. This was permanent.

No words of love had been exchanged, but they weren't really needed. She'd experienced enough to know that actions spoke louder than any word spoken.

Shailyn began to hum an old melody from one of her favorite movies as she began to unpack. She gathered up her scarves and looked back at the mirrored triple dresser, debating if maybe she should wait for him before choosing a drawer. She didn't feel comfortable moving his things. It occurred to her that she might not have to, considering the ease in which this transition had taken place.

She'd just opened the top drawer located on the left-hand side of the dresser when the soothing sound of the shower came from the bathroom. Somehow, it wasn't surprising that the drawer was completely empty except for one fine French lavender sachet just like the ones she used to keep in her drawers when they met. Another flame of affection ignited in her soul at his thoughtfulness.

He'd been so sure of her answer.

He'd been so sure of her, even when she'd doubted herself.

HE GRIMACED AT the filthy furniture spread out in front of him. This place had been a last resort, of sorts. This was much worse than the rural cabin and its simple homespun décor. He'd never intended to use this dwelling as temporary housing. It was a place he used for nothing more than storing needed supplies. It brought back memories he'd rather soon forget. He wiped his fingers on his khaki pants before pushing his glasses up the bridge of his nose.

The staleness of the old house made it rather stifling, but it would have to do for now.

Calvert had somehow discovered the treehouse over a hundred yards away from the cabin. The man had resources at his disposal, but it still should have taken him and the men working for his agency longer to connect the dots than it had.

Though this predicament did cause discomfort by forcing him to stay in this squalor, it proved once again that Calvert was the perfect adversary. He was more than capable.

He was now forced to prove Shailyn Doyle was alive.

The path to that resolution would be rather unpleasant considering he preferred to kill in a specific fashion, up close and personal. He suppressed the frustration that was trying to take hold in his immediate situation. That would only please Townes Calvert, and that wouldn't do.

He would make himself a cup of tea, drawing on the resources he'd compiled much earlier while he thought through his decision.

After all, killing for necessity over enjoyment was rather distasteful to everyone involved.

CHAPTER EIGHTEEN

TOWNES SENSED THE change in her breathing as she lay against him.

He didn't have to look at the bedside clock to know that it was only zero four hundred, give or take a few minutes. Shailyn had gotten roughly three hours of sleep. It was not nearly as much rest as he would have preferred her to have.

She shifted so that she was lying on her back. He waited patiently to see if she would slip back into a somewhat more peaceful slumber. There had been a short period where he'd considered waking her when she'd become restless, but drawing her body close to his had settled her.

She'd unpacked what things she'd brought with her before he ever stepped out of the bathroom, even going so far as to hang up a few blouses in the empty side of the closet next to his dress shirts. It had been satisfying to know she was in the other room aligning her things opposite his. He'd taken a long shower, giving her the time she needed to adjust to the change. No transformations were made without a few bumps along the way.

He made it a point not to talk about her parents' visit, nor the fact that Brody had to pull aside Dr. Carter Doyle to explain why Townes couldn't join them. He'd wanted her to have this time with them alone, anyway. It was too bad that Moss had gone and ruined the much overdue reunion.

"Why aren't you sleeping?"

Townes smirked, knowing full well she was looking at him. He never even attempted to shut off the bedside lamp. Honestly, he didn't care if they slept with the light on for the rest of their lives. She was lying next to him. That was all that mattered to either of them.

"I'll sleep when you sleep." Maybe that would give her incentive to try and get more than two or three hours at a stretch. He should have been more prepared for the mental scars left behind from her ordeal. Pure evil had touched her soul. It wasn't something one could shake off like the cold. "Come here."

Townes pulled her close once more, finally opening his eyes to see that she was indeed wide awake. She was studying him quite intently. It was more than apparent she wanted to ask him something.

"Do you need the light off to sleep?"

"Nope."

Townes lightly stroked her back over the long-sleeved shirt she'd chosen to sleep in. It was easy to see she craved warmth, as well as felt more comfortable in clothes that covered her scars. She would eventually learn that he could care less about the marks on her body. All that the raised ridges and blemishes reminded him of was her inner strength.

"Do you think he's going to leave Florida?"

She didn't have to clarify who she was talking about.

"No, I don't."

He didn't bother to add on *not without you.*

"Would you please shut off the light?"

Townes stopped moving his hand as he listened closely to the hitch in her breath. The last thing he would ever do was rush her for something she wasn't ready to give. He was perfectly content holding her against him. Her mere presence was more than enough to satisfy his voracious needs.

"Nope."

Shailyn tensed her body in response to his answer. She'd taken it wrong.

Townes very carefully shifted her so that she was once again on her back. She'd gathered her auburn hair into a ponytail so that the strands didn't get tangled while she slept, though a few wisps of bangs had escaped. He took his time brushing them away from her cheek as he settled himself between her legs.

Her eyes widened when she realized how much he wanted her. His erection was more than obvious.

"When you're ready."

Townes had refrained from kissing her the way he'd wanted to for fear she would turn away. So much had happened in the time they were apart, but also the time they were together. He needed her to experience safety and truly believe that he would lay his life down for her should the need arise.

"And if I'm ready now?"

She wasn't, but her question told him that she wanted more than a warm embrace.

Townes didn't break their gaze as he slowly lowered his lips to hers. She was holding her breath, but not for the reasons he thought. This was evident in the lone tear that slid down her face and into her hair.

He'd been wrong. It was intimacy she needed, and he'd been the one holding back.

"I've got you, freckles," Townes whispered against her cheek as he kissed away her tear. The taste of the salty moisture caused his chest to tighten in pain. "I've got every part of you."

Townes didn't rush this reintroduction to their familiarity. He took his time brushing his lips against every mark visible on her neck. He yearned to reach those areas on her soul which he knew were marred, but he was just a simple man, really.

From the curve of her jaw down to the camber of her collarbone, he showed her that the marks didn't matter. He ran his hands down her sides until his fingers slid underneath the bottom of her shirt. Her skin was still cool to the touch, but she would warm in time.

Three inches of her flawed abdomen were exposed, but he didn't hesitate to lean down and rest his cheek against the pale blemishes. She instinctively grabbed his shoulders to prevent him from revealing more of her body. He didn't allow that to stop him as he turned his head and placed his lips across an old burn mark that most likely had no sensation.

"Townes, you don't have to—"

"Shhh." Townes went from scar to scar, proving to her that each mark was to be revered. "Let me love you."

The catch in her throat was unmistakable. He didn't veer from his objective, though. Little by little, he continued to shift the soft material until he gently signaled that he wanted her to lift her arms. She did so willingly. Her breathing had become somewhat uneven at having her breasts exposed.

"You're beautiful," Townes whispered against the ample flesh. The wounds were bountiful, but so were the sexy freckles that no one would ever be able to rid her of no matter what was done to her skin. He'd thought of these abundant freckles often over the years. "You're absolutely gorgeous, freckles."

He kissed every exposed part of her upper body, leaving her hardened nipples for last. He caressed his thumb over her left nub as he took the other in his mouth, using his tongue to stroke over the sensitive area. Her grip continued to tighten on his hair the longer he took his time in pleasuring her.

"More, Townes," Shailyn appealed as she leaned her head

back against the pillow. The need lacing her tone was evident. His body responded to hers, but he wouldn't rush this long overdue reunification. "Please."

"I'd give you the moon if I had the ability," Townes murmured against her lips, as he lifted his upper body to steal another kiss before removing the black leggings that encased her legs. The golden hue of the bedside lamp darkened the pale scars left behind from a time that would never be forgotten. That didn't mean he wouldn't try to erase those memories with ones wrought with affection. "Close your eyes, freckles. Feel my touch on your body."

Townes started on the outside of her right thigh, taking time to kiss away whatever pain remained from each raised mark. Time continued to slip away as he loved her the way he'd longed for over the intervening years.

The sweet whimpers that escaped her lips were just as stimulating as the raspy moans emanating from her throat further on. Each tantalizing sound traveled through him until he was fully hard and wanting to enter her body. Still, he took his time until there was only one part of her that remained untouched.

Townes gently spread her legs to see her glistening folds. Shailyn had long ago released her hold on him when he'd been concentrating on her ankles and calves. He could see that she'd taken hold of the pillow in accepting her pleasure.

"Look at me." Shailyn fluttered her lashes before allowing him to see those emerald green eyes of hers that had turned dark as the seaweed swaying on the bottom of the ocean. He'd see to it that she had the freedom to dance in the water without fear of being taken away by the tide. No matter the consequences, he would make that a reality once she was free of her tormenter. "You are beautiful."

"I'm yours. Take me however you want."

There was a pause between her first two words, but it wasn't in hesitancy. It was more as if she'd wanted to add the word *finally*. She was absolutely right.

"You have always been mine to take."

SHAILYN HAD NEVER experienced being loved in this manner...not even during their previous time together.

She could attribute it to the fact that they'd both grown in their own ways, but that would be a lie. Every touch, every stroke, and every caress made an imprint on her that would forever alter the way she saw herself.

It was almost impossible to lay there while he ran his tongue through her folds, but she wouldn't deny herself his love. There would be time for words later...time to express what was in her heart. His gentle touch told her all she needed to know for now.

The ache had started as a low pulse, but she was now throbbing to the point of pain. She needed him inside of her. She needed him to take her to that place she remembered in those few dreams that her mind still allowed her to hold onto in between the nightmares. It had been the reason she'd been able to save her sanity.

The moment his finger gradually entered her was the instant her vision burst into tiny flashes. It wasn't enough to send her completely over that precipice, but it was sufficient enough to start the journey over the edge.

"Townes, I need—"

"Keep your legs spread," Townes whispered firmly, adding another finger so that her sheath had something more substantial to grip. He was resolute in his inclination to take her to the edge and back. She was going to die from her want of more pleasure. It was most preferable to the other death she'd anticipated. "Just feel."

There had been parts to Shailyn that had lost sensation, but she couldn't begin to locate those areas. Her entire body was getting ready to shatter, and all she could do was prepare for the ultimate detonation.

His lips closed around the sensitive ball of nerves at the apex of her folds. He gently suckled until her inner thighs shook with anticipation. A sharp zing of intense rapture shot through her core unexpectedly. Endless contractions took hold and by the time she could draw air, he'd donned protection.

His engorged tip was now at her entrance.

He slowly filled her to the point of a burn that she had no doubt would become addictive in the days, weeks, months, and years to come. Only when he was almost fully seated deep within her did he gather her in his arms and roll over onto his back, positioning her to take that last inch.

"I've always been yours."

Townes expressed those words with sincerity, but she was aware of the double meaning behind them. She gazed into his grey eyes and lost her soul in their depths as she took them both on another journey that led them into a welcoming nirvana.

HE HAD COME to a decision.

It was one that would guarantee him the victory.

Or it could very well end his somewhat diverting life as the world's most notorious serial killer.

CHAPTER NINETEEN

"**T**HE BURNT BODY Moss left behind at the cabin was his twin brother."

Half the team was gathered around the table, though Keane and Royce had joined them via phone. The grey receiver sat in the middle of a small conference table in the back of Brody's domain, but the silence from everyone listening to such a bombshell came through loud and clear.

"The small percentile difference in their DNA accounted for a recessive pigmentation gene. He was an albino with what was suspected to be another common defect associated with that condition—he was most likely blind. The burns made it impossible to visually identify Moss' body at the scene. It only became obvious after an expert reviewed the DNA evidence and issued his findings. A subsequent review of the autopsy findings confirmed the eyes were burned beyond recognition, but upon a secondary examination…the ocular nerves had been damaged when he was younger. It's not believed that his blindness was due to his albino condition. Apparently, the damage was caused by a traumatic physical incident, possibly from an altercation."

Townes had spent a good two hours in front of the white board he'd constructed in his office. It had taken him a rather long time to put together a timeline. Each member on this team had contributed with each piece of information they'd uncovered over the last four to five months.

Every moment in Moss' life, as well as anyone who he'd had contact with, had been outlined. It was a tree of secrets, of sorts. One person stood out above the rest—his mother.

The frayed end of the string that contained her history had almost been nonexistent. Nonetheless, it had been there. All it had needed was a little tug.

Beatrice Moss had hidden Shepherd Moss' brother from the world.

"Where the hell did you come up with this scenario?" Brody was currently sitting on his preferred stool that allowed him to wheel back and forth between the papers laid out in front of everyone to his handcrafted desk where there were various feeds from the wooded area Moss last occupied. "Moss didn't have a brother last week."

"He didn't have any siblings we were aware of," Sawyer corrected, lowering his mug before he managed to take a sip of coffee. He tapped on one of the files in front of him to stress his point. "According to the townsfolk, Moss was the only child to a single mother who struggled to make ends meet. They lived pretty far out in the country. It's sounding to me that this brother was an embarrassment to the family name."

"You're right." Townes didn't dispute the facts that had been laid out to them, but he led his team directly to the oversight they'd all missed during the subsequent trial to put Moss behind bars. Looking back, there hadn't been a reason to delve into the man's childhood. Townes had personally ensured that a guilty verdict came through without doubt. The prosecutor had been given a slam dunk case and extensive research wasn't really needed. "Beatrice Moss was a single mother who had gone without a formal education. She struggled to make ends meet her whole life. No one noticed the absent birth certificate. The twins were a home birth, using an old-fashioned midwife. There was never any record of a twin brother. The family hid the poor child on the family's tenement farm that Moss must have bought for his mother and brother to live out their days on after he'd gotten work in the city."

No one was to blame for overlooking a poor woman's life that amounted to nothing, who in theory had not been in the picture for a number of years. She'd passed away of heart failure during Moss' stint in federal prison. There wasn't even a record of where she was buried. The team had tried to search for family connections to the body presumed to be Moss at the cabin, but they had been searching in the wrong direction. It was no one's fault.

"Beatrice Moss never attended school as a child, which was quite common in that area during those years. Her family was poor and subsisted off the farmland." Townes shot a glance at Coen, who had been the one to piece together a timeline of Moss' history due to past interviews Moss had granted during his incarceration. "For a young girl with such low expectations, ending up as a waitress for the local diner barely making ends meet didn't seem so unusual. She taught herself to read and write. She lived her entire life in the backwoods, only coming into town to work her shift and disappearing back into the woods afterward."

"That's not unusual in a lot of small towns all over this country." Keane had responded with what everyone was thinking. "Money was scarce. Her parents were older and needed help around the house. Some guy made nice during one of her shifts and didn't stick around longer than it took to get into her panties."

"All true, which is why Beatrice didn't tell her parents that she was pregnant till it was too late. That's why she ended up with just a midwife." Townes broke down the timeline, grateful that Shailyn had stayed up at the main house. He needed to pay a visit with her parents sometime today. He needed to explain the delicacy of this part of the investigation. Their cooperation was needed to ensure their daughter's life wasn't needlessly endangered. "I made a couple of phone calls first thing this morning to some relatives I believe had the ability to help Beatrice after her parents passed. It turns out a long distant cousin who was in her mid-thirties had seen both children on the farm during the time when she had visited—one of them being fair complexioned."

"What a lovely family," Brody said wryly, shaking his head at this breakthrough. He rolled over to one of the monitors not in use, moving the mouse to activate the screen. "I'll see if I can obtain a name. I'll track down whatever dental records there might have been and send them over to the lab to make a confirmation, if I can."

"I want this leaked to the press immediately."

Townes had spent a lot of time trying to figure out a way to flush Moss out of hiding. The man was too intelligent to make rash decisions, but a few pushes would lead the man in the right direction. A collision with reality was a foregone conclusion.

"Royce, I'm going to have Caitlyn pull a few strings to get this story front and center this evening. I want him to feel the pressure and know that we're one step closer." Townes went down the list on what he wanted each team member to do today while he visited Carter and Pam Doyle. That was one meeting he would have to handle personally. "Any questions?"

"What's the end game?" Coen leaned back in his chair and surveyed Townes with curiosity. "How are we going to draw Moss out of hiding without using Shailyn?"

"I've learned something over the course of this investigation that wasn't relevant at the time of Moss' trial." Townes gestured toward the numerous files on the table. "He liked to physically watch the aftermath of his crimes. From the few conversations I've had with him on the phone, he's had information acquired by the news. He also stayed up in that hidden treehouse while every law enforcement agency combed through the wreckage he'd left behind. He enjoyed watching the show below as if he were a puppet master and we were nothing more than his puppets on a string for him to make dance."

This was the reason it was so vital he speak with Carter and Pam Doyle.

"We're going to use Shailyn's funeral service as a web, similar to what we had planned before. We'll draw him in closer using the media, but there isn't a chance in hell he's going to miss an opportunity to see if her body is the one laying inside that coffin. He won't pass this one off to some follower."

"It was never announced to the media where her body was being held," Brody said over his shoulder. "We can have Caitlyn call up Maura Jane, who's been the lead anchor covering the story, and drop a hint as to which funeral home the Doyle's have chosen and when the Marshals Service is releasing the body to them for burial. A staged funeral might not need to be necessary if Moss has a more private venue to confirm Shailyn's death."

"I thought of that, but he's far too careful. He'll believe it's a setup if we make it too obvious. He'll hire someone to go to the funeral and acquire pictures of the open casket, all the while keeping his distance because of the close quarters." Townes hated that the need for a theatrical performance was required, but he could see no other way to draw Moss out from hiding. "A cemetery can offer Moss anonymity while providing him freedom to move about. He'll use that to his advantage. He'll want to be there in person. The churchyard the Doyle's use for their family plots has mature trees, as well as numerous large tombs and above ground crypts. He'll use those elements for concealment, allowing him to personally say goodbye to his greatest unfinished masterpiece."

"The Doyles were supposed to meet with the funeral director today at fifteen hundred hours," Brody informed them, though Townes was already aware of their schedule. "His name is Donald Barnaby."

"The federal offices in Portland handled his call as to when Shailyn's body would be available for release, saying sometime later this week."

"I'll take care of the family details." Townes had a busy day, but he first needed to don a suit and then speak to Shailyn. As of today, the oncoming events would occur at a rapid rate. He wanted her prepared, but he also needed to know she was ready for the possible outcome. "Sawyer and Coen, I want the two of you to take lead on securing the personnel needed for this operation. Use your discretion as to who to bring in from the funeral home, as well as the cemetery grounds. I want this net airtight."

"Royce and I intended to interview Lucas Grove again later this morning. We're all in agreement that a twelve-year-old boy could never have been able to carry out the murder of Caroline Marinovic alone," Keane said, his voice drifting through the phone receiver. "We're going to press him hard for some answers."

"Do what you have to. Push the envelope," Townes granted, having full faith that Keane and Royce understood the boundaries of such an interview.

It didn't take him long to leave the major portion of the preparation for the upcoming operation in his team's hands. He walked into the main house to see Brett and Camryn wrapping

Christmas presents and humming along to Christmas carols as if this were any other ordinary holiday season. Shailyn was standing in the kitchen, looking on with desire to join in.

"Good morning," Remy called out, her blonde hair pulled back in a twist with one strand left out to frame her face. The grey business suit gave away her destination. "I need to head into the office for the holiday luncheon. Does anyone need anything while I'm in the city?"

A few items were thrown out; mainly another round of wrapping paper, bows, and tape requested. Brett had grabbed a piece of paper and jotted down the list. Remy took it, along with her briefcase she'd carried into the kitchen, and proceeded to the patio door.

"See you guys later," Remy called out, slowing her pace as she walked past Townes. "I was able to secure that item you requested. Delivery is Christmas morning."

Remy winked at him as he opened the sliding glass door, allowing her to step out into the morning sunshine. It was a rather cool day, though. December temperatures always tended to bring a little chill with it. He had no doubt that she was heading to the main outbuilding to say goodbye to Brody.

"Good morning." Townes brushed past Shailyn, directly meeting her gaze. She smiled over the rim of her coffee cup. He reached for the white porcelain one next to the carafe. "Do you have a minute? I need to discuss a few things with you."

"I have a lifetime of minutes," Shailyn confessed, her cheeks turning the color of her hair when Camryn didn't even bother to cover up her laugh. She mumbled an apology before using the scissors to strip a line of ribbon, causing the material to curl. "Speaking of which, we never really discussed my teaching position."

Townes winced at where this conversation was heading, not

bothering to cover up his facial expression. Her sigh was audible and accepting at the same time. Everyone thought she was dead, so there was nothing for her to do until Moss was brought into custody or planted in the Florida DOC cemetery.

"I'm sure your position will be given back to you once we explain to the college administration the unique circumstances you were encumbered by." Townes ignored another chuckle from Camryn, though he did appreciate her attempt at keeping some humor injected into the situation. "Let's go into my office. I want to discuss something with you in private."

Shailyn straightened her shoulders as if he were about to tell her the world was coming to an end. He loathed that she automatically assumed the worst. She searched his body language for what could possibly have happened in the course of the hour he'd been with the team.

"It's just an update, freckles. It's nothing too dire."

Townes poured the coffee into his mug, already thinking he should have taken the time to make his special blend in the office. Unfortunately, he wasn't going to be around to enjoy it. He set the carafe back in place when he realized that it was too quiet. He picked up his mug and turned to find Brett and Camryn staring at him from their seats at the table.

He'd called Shailyn by her nickname in front of them. He'd fallen back into an old routine, but he refused to apologize for it. These women had only ever saw him a certain way, mostly due to his role in this company. That didn't mean he would forego the intimacy that had grown between him and Shailyn.

"I'm heading over to your parents' house. There are some things I need to discuss with them," Townes explained quietly, resting his hand on Shailyn's lower back. He guided her out of the kitchen, down the hallway, and steered her toward the staircase instead of his office. "I'm running low on time, so we'll have to talk as I'm getting ready."

"What you're wearing is fine." Shailyn shot him a sideways glance. It was more than apparent she thought he was changing his clothes because of the upcoming confrontation with her father. That was far from the case. He was very comfortable with who he was as a man. He had nothing to prove, and Carter Doyle certainly wasn't the reason he needed to don a suit. "Is there a reason my parents can't come here?"

"I know you'd like to see them again, but we can't risk Moss thinking that you're here and very much alive." Townes continued to guide Shailyn down the long hallway to where their bedroom was located. He'd waited a long time to have this sense of home. There wasn't a chance in hell he would risk having it taken away. "Which is why I'm going to have your parents continue to plan your funeral service."

"That is a bit morbid," Shailyn expressed with a hint of despair. She moved through the room and sat on the edge of the bed as he made his way to their walk-through closet. "So that's it? We're just going to hope he believes I'm dead and moves on?"

"No, not at all." Townes removed his holster, using one of the various hooks on the wall for a temporary holder. How could he explain what was about to take place without adding to her stress? He removed his t-shirt and then glanced over toward the bed. "We're setting up a sting. We're using your funeral as bait."

"Because Moss will want to see my dead body for himself. Please tell me I won't have to lie in a coffin to make this believable."

The sadness in her voice caused his chest to tighten. This was exactly why he'd wanted to have this conversation in private. He quickly switched out his jeans for his dress pants before taking a white dress shirt off the hanger. He walked into the bedroom with every intention of altering how she viewed the upcoming days.

"Moss needs to see you, Shailyn. You are all he's thought of every day in that cell for years. He would have preferred to be with you when you took your last breath, but for some reason it's vital he say his final goodbyes in person."

Shailyn had laid down on the made bed, the white scarf around her neck stark against the dark color of the comforter. She was staring at the ceiling, but her emerald green eyes averted to his as he leaned over her to stress his point.

"Moss *will* show up at your funeral. When he does, we'll be there to end this."

Townes brushed aside a strand of her auburn hair. She had always been his everything. No one would take away what they'd finally reclaimed...not even Moss.

SHAILYN STARED UP into those grey eyes that she'd dreamed of last night and this morning, wishing the fear that had gripped her since waking would fade into oblivion. Townes had been in the shower when she'd jolted awake and sought his warmth. His side of the bed had been cold from his absence.

They'd made love...beautiful love. He'd spent hours kissing every mark, blemish, and scar that marked her body. She understood that he'd done so to prove to her he wasn't bothered by the multitude of distortions Moss had left on her body.

It was her soul that worried her most.

"Why can't we just stay here for the rest of our lives?" Shailyn whispered, reaching up with her right hand and pressing it against his cheek imploringly. He was leaning over her without a shirt. Did he think that his masculinity didn't affect her? It took everything in her not to touch him the way she wanted. "I don't think I ever thanked you for what you created here."

"I can think of many ways you can do exactly that, but right now all I need is your promise that you'll stay here while the team and I see this investigation through to the end." Townes rested his elbow on the bed as he slowly leaned down and kissed her thoroughly. He took his time and never once made her think he was needed elsewhere. "Is there anything you need?"

There were a lot of things she needed, but he was already working on that list. She forced a smile and shook her head, déjà vu settling in when he pulled away. Her nightmare returned with a vengeance.

"Freckles?"

"Here," Shailyn said, clearing her throat and using his hand as leverage to move off the bed. She took his shirt and held it open, prompting him to slip his arms into the sleeves. Her small diversion didn't work from the way he raised his eyebrow. "Will you tell my parents that I love them?"

"Of course, I will." Townes allowed her to fasten each button on his dress shirt, though he was watching her closely. "You can tell them yourself when this is all said and done."

Shailyn finished her task and then stepped back, allowing him to tuck the dress shirt into his black pants. She resisted the urge to wrap her arms around her waist for fear he would question her further, but she didn't want to add more to his already full plate. She walked to the window, adjusting the security shutter so that a little bit of sunshine came through the slats.

Did you think that I wouldn't get retribution?

Moss held the same knife in his hand that he'd used to torture her with all those years ago. Townes was on his knees, bloody and bruised. The knife was at his throat.

"You don't get to live your life without me, Shailyn."

Shailyn was startled when Townes began to list the things he had on his agenda for the day. His voice had chased away the visions from her nightmare this morning.

Unfortunately, she couldn't shake the feeling that the fates had another itinerary for them.

"IN AN UPDATE on the Shepherd Moss investigation, it appears the parents of Shailyn Doyle will be holding her funeral the morning of Christmas Eve. It's a tragedy what Carter and Pam Doyle have endured during..."

He peered down at the sightless eyes staring up at him in what appeared to be shock. Death shouldn't have come as a surprise, though it was understandable given past events.

Maybe a message would be beneficial. It would be broadcasted so that his followers understood what happened when he was betrayed.

He knelt beside the body and dragged a finger through the pooling blood. He didn't like to kill simply for the sake of killing. There was no pleasure if there was no pain inflicted. It didn't take long to write the one word that would capture Townes Calvert's attention.

Caroline.

CHAPTER TWENTY

"How sure are you that this plan of yours will work?"

Townes didn't reply to Carter Doyle's question right away as he mulled over the best way to answer. He casually peered out the glass window that was basically an entire wall facing the ocean. He'd known which location to drive to based on the security detail he'd put on Shailyn's parents the moment Moss escaped federal prison.

"Carter, he's doing everything he—"

"This is our only daughter, Pam!" Carter had raised his voice to get his point across, but all it did was prove to Townes that the doctor had let emotion cloud his judgment. "He took her out of WITSEC where she was safe. He has placed her life in even more danger than before, if that's even possible."

"I have no doubt that Moss would have eventually discovered Shailyn's new identity and location. It was only a matter of time. I took every step necessary to ensure her safety."

Townes had already gone over his reasoning with the Doyles as to why he'd manufactured Shailyn's death and moved her to a new location with increased security. He would do so again and again if it meant he could get them on board with what needed to be done.

He faced Carter and Pam, addressing the one topic they had

all avoided.

"I understand that I'm not your first choice for Shailyn. But you need to understand that we love each other, and I would lay down my life for her." Townes' phone vibrated, but he ignored whatever text had come through as he explained in detail what would happen after this investigation was closed...either with Moss behind bars awaiting the death penalty after being convicted of his most recent string of crimes...or dead. "This is our best chance to capture Moss. I'm asking on Shailyn's behalf that you continue to plan her funeral and have it in two days' time so that we all have the opportunity to live out our lives without Moss' presence. Should things go according to plan, it's only fair you understand that I intend to ask Shailyn for her hand in marriage."

Townes wasn't surprised when Carter turned away in frustration, but he was taken aback when Pam stood from her seat on the couch. She crossed the tiled floor and reached for his hands, which he held out for her to grasp.

"Townes, it's not that we don't believe you're good enough for Shailyn. We thought it best at the time that you stay away from her, because I don't doubt that she would never have entered the witness protection program if you hadn't. She loved you back then, and I know that love hasn't faded." Pam swallowed, giving herself time to compose herself as tears filled her eyes. "One day, when you have children, you'll understand just how hard it was for us to see her go away. She was—is—our world. All we've ever wanted was her happiness. You give that to her, just as you have proven what lengths you've gone to in order to bring her back to all of us. You have our blessing to marry our daughter, Townes."

This wasn't the conversation Townes had intended to have, but he was a firm believer in utilizing the paths provided. Dr.

Doyle was rubbing the back of his neck in annoyance. He clearly wasn't ready to have this discussion.

"Calvert, do you recall how we met?"

Townes vividly remembered how the two of them had crossed paths.

"The life you saved was a twenty-two-year-old boy who'd gotten mixed up with the wrong group of people. One percenters aren't known for being the most law-abiding group, but there were reasons I ran with that crowd after I finished serving my country." Townes wouldn't defend his actions to a civilian, but he would respect the father of the woman he intended to marry. He and Shailyn hadn't discussed their future in detail, but it was a given. "I respect everyone's choice to choose their own way of life and the reasons behind their decisions are their own. No one is better than anyone else because they were born to privilege. Some of those very men you look down your nose at are the very ones risking their lives to ensure your daughter's safety."

"You think I don't grasp the risk you and your men are taking for Shailyn?" Carter walked to the wet bar and poured himself a double scotch. It had always been his preferred drink, though it was rather early in the day to be pouring that heavy. Townes didn't begrudge him the alcohol, though. He was technically getting ready to bury his daughter, and he certainly needed to act the part. "You seem to forget that I helped that young man without question."

Carter had already called in that chip when it came time to protect his daughter. The good doctor finally turned to face Townes, but there wasn't disdain written across his features the way he'd assumed. There was only a helplessness that he could relate too.

"Our daughter means more to us than anything else in this world, Calvert." Dr. Doyle raised his glass in salute, but he downed the liquid for courage against the days ahead. "Her happiness means our happiness."

Townes would take that as Carter's blessing. With that out of the way, a few more details were discussed that would be needed in order to pull off the funeral. Brody would take care of the majority of the responsibilities as far as making arrangements with the funeral home. There could be no mistakes at this point.

Another thirty or so minutes passed before he was able to leave the premises without bloodshed. He'd missed two calls from Brody and one from Keane. A couple texts summed up what Brody wanted to convey, but Keane's was rather vague.

"What have you got?" Townes asked as he opened his car door. The modest sedan had been courtesy of the U.S. Marshals Service, along with a title that served his purpose when needed. He did his job to the best of his ability, but the reasoning behind such a position was because of one woman. "And make it brief. I'm about to meet with Agent Gordon."

"Lucas Grove is dead."

Townes had just pressed the ignition button when the words penetrated his conscious thoughts. He took a moment to think through what this meant and came to the conclusion Moss had to have had a valid reason for going to such lengths.

"How, where, and when?"

Townes rolled down the window on the driver's side door to get some fresh air. It was stifling hot with this black leather interior. He looked in the rearview mirror to see the security detail assigned to the Doyles.

"Grove's throat was slit." Keane was brief and to the point. "The word *Caroline* was written in blood on the hardwood floor next to his body."

It was highly doubtful Grove had written his former fiancée's name while he was bleeding out.

"Moss is cleaning up house."

That could only mean that they were getting close to finding out who murdered Caroline Marinovic. There was no doubt that Moss was involved, even at the young age of twelve. Something occurred to Townes just then. What if Moss' brother had been involved?

"Why not eliminate Grove when Moss left him in the Everglades? Why not wrap up loose ends then?"

"Because Moss was only delaying him until he could manage the task himself," Townes surmised, a little bit of the puzzle falling into place. He shifted the gear into reverse, slowly backing out of the driveway. "Tear apart Grove's house, his classroom, and anywhere else he spent his time. See if there is any evidence to support Moss was involved."

A twelve-year-old boy with the high intelligence Moss exhibited could have easily conned an adult male into aiding and abetting him or them. Caroline Marinovic had been the start of Moss' sick and twisted vocation. The question remained…what had she done to trigger his malevolent thoughts, causing them to become reality?

"I'll be in touch."

Townes disconnected the line and didn't bother to connect his Bluetooth in the vehicle to reach Brody.

"I'm already on it," Brody exclaimed, his voice all but drifting out the window as Townes shifted the sedan into drive. He had around a thirty-minute trip into the city. "The camera access of the street Grove lived on doesn't have enough coverage of the backyards. I'll pick through some satellite feeds, but I think I may have figured out where Moss went after leaving the secondary cabin location."

"Where?" Townes was more than willing to change his plans should Brody come up with a valid location on Moss' current whereabouts.

"I directed Royce over to Moss' childhood farm. After doing some digging into the real estate there, I discovered the neighbor who lived on that same rural route had died a couple of years back. The property is in foreclosure and has basically been left abandoned."

Townes had security details on numerous people who Moss might reach out to under this type of law enforcement pressure, as well as places he might want to revisit. His childhood home had been sold after his mother's passing to a family of three. The local sheriff had scheduled regular patrols through the area, but it wasn't in Moss' nature to target families needlessly. Besides, he wouldn't return there and potentially expose himself without reason.

A rundown home that was in foreclosure, though? Another knot started to unravel. Had Moss' brother used that dwelling to have a roof over his head after the family land was sold?

"I figured it was worth a shot." Brody had made the right call directing Royce there instead of Coen or Sawyer, both of whom were busy setting up the operation at the graveyard. "I take it you're done talking to the Doyles?"

"Yes. It went better than expected."

Townes held his cell between his ear and shoulder as he pressed the button that would roll up the window. The air had finally kicked on and was creating a comfortable atmosphere inside the sedan. He pulled the car to a stop at the intersection, switching his turn signal on to indicate a left-hand turn.

"I'm heading toward—"

The sudden and deafening boom that ricocheted through Townes' ears was nothing compared to the jarring impact his body suffered from the collision of another oncoming vehicle from behind. The back and side windows imploded all at once, showering him with miniscule shards of safety glass. His neck snapped back with the force from the blow.

There was no reaction time. It was all impact.

Gravity and energy had taken over as their way in the world of physics.

His face took the blunt force of the airbag when his body jerked forward and the white powdered material exploded from the steering wheel. The meeting of metal on metal had dealt the blow that was entirely predictable. The seatbelt barred his body from flying through the windshield, but the safety harness wasn't capable of preventing the darkness from taking over.

CHAPTER TWENTY-ONE

S HAILYN COULDN'T PREVENT a bright spark of hope from forming once she'd heard about the thread Brody had just located amongst the carnage. At least, that's how Townes always referred to a lead.

What if this thin strand actually led them back to Moss?

"I figured it was worth a shot," Brody said to Townes as he began to pull up images from what appeared to be a grainy video feed. She assumed it was from the area Moss had grown up, but she didn't know how it might help them catch a killer. "I take it you're done talking to the Doyles?"

Shailyn had been wondering all morning how her parents would take Townes' request to keep up the pretense of her death. They'd been told by Brody how important it was to the investigation, but she highly doubted they would be so agreeable to put their extended family and friends through such an experience.

She'd looked into the soulless eyes of that sadistic man. There was no telling what he might do to exact revenge for her untimely death.

"Calvert?"

Brody's concerned tone had Shailyn dragging her gaze away from the large monitor. He slowly stood, causing the stool to gradually move away from him. Nausea rolled her stomach when she recognized that look of alarm.

Something had happened to Townes.

Something bad.

Shailyn involuntarily grabbed Brody's arm, trying to get him to look at her and explain what was going on.

"Calvert, are you alright?"

Her mind spun in so many directions with what could have happened to Townes, but he was with her parents. Wait. No, he wasn't. Brody had mentioned that their conversation was over, which could only mean that Townes was either driving to his next meeting or something had happened at the field office in Orlando.

"Brody, what's happened?" Shailyn asked desperately, unable to keep the tremor from her voice. She didn't care. "Is Townes hurt?"

Brody didn't answer her, but instead started tapping away at his keyboard. It was more like pounding, but it got the job done. A satellite image appeared on the screen with a flashing blue circle.

"Fuck," Brody exclaimed in annoyance, quickly setting the cell phone he'd been using down on the desk. The landline was in his other hand before she realized what he was doing. "I need an ambulance and fire personnel at..."

Brody rapidly gave the 911 operator the cross streets to Townes' location. She still couldn't figure out what he assumed had happened, but she kept telling herself over and over that it had nothing to do with Moss. A part of her was relieved when Brody hung up and told her what he believed had happened, but in no way did his opinion lessen her worry over Townes' wellbeing.

"I think Calvert was in an automobile accident." Brody was

now texting messages without breaking stride. She figured he was notifying the team, but he was apparently doing more than that. "There was a security detail near your parents' beach house. Those two are nearest Calvert's location, so I'm having one of them head that way now."

She didn't have to be told this could all be a ruse to reach her parents, but the likelihood of that was low. Moss could have gotten to them if he desired without so much as a trace of his presence showing up until their detail missed their check-in time slot. No one was willing to take that chance, though.

"I want to go." Shailyn was already aware of Brody's answer before he ever moved his lips. "Please."

"I'm sorry, Shailyn, you know I can't allow that to happen." Brody quickly reached for his firearm, which wasn't contained in a shoulder holster like the majority of the team wore. Instead, his holster attached to the waist of his cargo shorts. His Hawaiian shirt fell back into place with a slight difference. "There are twenty sentries roaming this property. No one is getting in or out. You're safe here."

Shailyn wanted to tell him that he didn't have to clarify why she couldn't leave. She'd been told enough times and had lived through the consequences once before. She wasn't looking to repeat her past experiences.

"Do you still have the phone I provided you?" Brody asked, ignoring the ringing of his cell. She had no doubt that it was the rest of the team trying to get updates on what was happening. "Shailyn, please look at me."

Shailyn had been staring at the phone in his hand, willing him to answer it in case it was Townes. He moved in front of her until she had no choice but to look up into his concerned gaze. She curled her fingers into the palms of her hands to prevent herself from grabbing his arms and begging him to make this right.

"Keep that phone on you at all times." Brody rested a reassuring hand on her shoulder, but she barely noticed. She'd gone numb. "I'll call you with updates."

Shailyn hadn't even had time to turn and watch him leave. He was already out the door.

The hums of the various monitors were droning in the background, but she could still detect the shallowness of her breathing. She reached out for one of the various chairs around the office, lowering herself into the seat as she tried to piece together what had happened.

Townes had visited with her parents before driving into the city. He hadn't made it to his destination, because she'd recognized the cross streets Brody had given the 911 operator. He was still very near the beach.

What could possibly have caused the bad connection? What could have disconnected his call to Brody?

"Shailyn?"

She looked toward the door to find Brett and Camryn walking in, their concern palpable.

"They think Townes might have been in an accident," Shailyn shared, unable to keep the tremor out of her voice. She rested her fists in her lap and fought the urge to call her parents. They were close to the site. They would be able to tell her if Townes was okay. "He's so…"

"Indestructible?" Camryn offered up an adjective that fit, but Shailyn believed Townes was much more than that. "He's overly cautious and very aware of his surroundings. It could very well be nothing."

No one in this room believed whatever happened to Townes was an accident. Brody had left the compound. That, in and of itself, spoke volumes.

Shailyn needed a minute to think. Camryn and Brett continued to speak reassurances while the blue circle blinked
incessantly in its own rhythm every half second. Nothing helped.
The longer she stared at the monitor, the more her vision
tunneled to the point she was afraid she'd faint.

"Would you continue to watch that blue dot?" Shailyn asked
as she stood, all the while forcing her trembling legs to hold her
up. "I just need a bit of fresh air."

Shailyn made it across the room and through the door before either woman could recognize the physical state she was in.
She closed the door behind her, using its unyielding strength to
keep her upright. She closed her eyes and did her best to even
out her breathing.

An image of the intersection near her parents' home came to
mind. Why would Townes have lost cell service if he'd been in a
mere fender bender? She assumed he'd been using the Bluetooth
in the vehicle. Maybe the service was automatically disconnected
upon impact? Had Brody overreacted?

Shailyn sensed the vibration of the burner phone through
the back pocket of her jeans. She hadn't been lying when she'd
told Brody that she'd had the device on her person. She'd never
used it before now, though. He'd given it to her only in the case
of emergency, or so that Townes was able to reach her when he
was off the property. She was holding it to her ear before the
third cadence.

"Townes?"

There was silence on the other end. Shailyn quickly checked
the number on the display, but she didn't recognize it. She
wouldn't. This was a burner phone that had nothing stored in
memory.

"Hello?" Shailyn called out once more with a little less desperation. A bit of relief shot through her at the thought that

Townes *did* have a bad connection. "I don't know if you can hear me, but Brody is on his way."

"I'll make sure Townes knows just how much his team cares for him."

Shailyn almost dropped to her knees at the sound of a voice she still heard in her dreams. For one brief moment, she considered that maybe this was nothing but another nightmare.

"Shailyn, I need you to listen closely."

Moss' tone came across as if he were trying to soothe her, but it didn't matter how he spoke to her. She couldn't breathe. She was suffocating.

"W-what have you done?" she managed to say through the tight constriction of her throat. It felt like he was physically choking her. She fought back the urge to heave up the contents of her stomach.

"I did what was necessary to get you back," Moss exclaimed in a manner that indicated she should have already known that little detail. "Now we're wasting time. I don't have to tell you what will happen to your beloved one should you not do exactly as I say. You are to come alone to…"

Moss' voice droned on and on with explicit details while she did her best not to scream. She wiped away the continuous tears that were running down her cheeks, conscious of the pain this sadistic monster could inflict on Townes if she didn't follow through with his instructions. He would most likely do those vile things anyway. Any noncompliance would just make Townes' life end sooner.

Shailyn had truly thought she'd experienced the worst pain during those three endless days, but she'd been wrong. Physical pain had nothing over the emotional agony of knowing she was helpless to stop Moss from hurting Townes.

But she wasn't helpless.

"Shailyn, do you understand my instructions?"

"Yes." Her reply came out as a whisper. It hadn't been her intention, but it seemed to cause him happiness.

"Good." The tone Moss used imposed another round of nausea. "I look forward to seeing you again, Shailyn."

She pressed the phone hard against her forehead as she fought for composure. She failed, and yet she understood she would succeed. Sobs wracked her body until she was on the ground. She allowed the pain of the past, present, and future to crush her.

The overwhelming anguish was almost welcoming.

CHAPTER TWENTY-TWO

T HE BLINDING LIGHT only succeeded in causing the throbbing pain to become even more excruciating. It was as if his head had caught fire.

Townes remained still, trying to get a sense of his surroundings. His training tempered his reaction to the unknown. That had been drilled into him early on in his life before being reinforced by the military. He doubted anyone would have noticed the slight movement of his lashes.

The last thing he recalled was leaving the Doyle residence.

No, that wasn't right.

He'd been speaking with Brody on the phone regarding a lead Royce was going to follow up on. His memory began to return little by little, until he recalled being stopped at the intersection.

Someone had crashed into the back of his vehicle at a high rate of speed.

Townes strained to hear any sounds that would indicate he was in the hospital. There was no squeaking of soles on the tiled floor, no monitors beeping, and certainly no medical personnel shouting orders. The only thing he could make out were...birds?

At least another three minutes passed without hearing anything other than the rustling of leaves. He slowly opened his eyes to find the source of the light hanging directly overhead.

It was the sun.

The temperature was around seventy-four degrees, and though it was relatively cool considering the lower humidity this time of year, the heat radiating from the sun's rays was stifling.

Moving his head had the blood pounding painfully against his temples. The muscle strand on the right side of his neck protested the movement, as well.

Fuck.

Townes gritted his teeth at the effort it took him to move, but he finally managed to roll to his side and use his elbow as leverage. His hair fell into his eyes, signifying that he'd lost the elastic band he'd used this morning somewhere along the way.

Was he lying on dirt and rocks? Had he been thrown from the vehicle?

A quick glance around the immediate area caused him to realize that his first assumption wasn't accurate. He was in a stone pit, of sorts. The rattling of a chain caught his attention.

What the hell was around his ankle?

Townes quickly reached for the shackle that had been fastened around his right pant leg, ignoring the stinging sensation that had taken up residence in his left eye. His vision was semi-blurred, but that fact didn't stop him from seeing just how secure the metal clasp was locked into place.

There would be no easy way of getting the metal clamp off his leg without a key for the lock. He checked for his weapon knowing full well his firearm wouldn't be in his holster. To make matters worse, he wasn't even wearing his shoulder holster. Someone had removed it from his body.

Townes didn't have to guess as to who, but had it been by the man himself or by one of his acolytes?

"Son of a bitch."

Townes assumed Moss had caused the car accident, wanting some form of substitute for Shailyn. He wasn't looking forward to whatever the sadistic fuck had planned, but he'd take whatever Moss dished out as long as he continued to believe that Shailyn was dead.

"Moss!"

Townes listened intently for any sound that the man was near. The wildlife had fallen somewhat quiet at his exclamation, but there wasn't the crunch of the grass or a rustle of fabric to be heard.

Did Moss believe by making Townes wait for his ultimate torture that it would cause him to be more compliant?

That sure as hell wasn't going to happen, so Townes would use the time to formulate a plan of action. He wiped his left eye with the back of his hand, not surprised to come away with blood on his skin. Head wounds usually bled profusely.

Just how long had he been out here?

The team would have already casted a wide search net. Brody had been on the phone at the time of the accident. It wouldn't take him long to put two and two together, especially when Townes was no longer at the crash site.

He considered himself modest, but he did recognize his fortitude. He wasn't an easy man to take down. The crash had to be executed in a manner precise enough to make him lose consciousness, but not to the point where it was life-threatening.

Moss wouldn't have been involved. He had someone else initiate the crash and capitalized on the carnage.

Townes took stock of his surroundings once more. He was far enough away from civilization that it was doubtful anyone would hear him call out for help. This pit he was in was rather unusual. It looked to be maybe twelve feet wide and maybe seven feet deep. Large boulders were stacked on top of one another, almost as if it were some type of shrine. He could easily have removed himself from this cavity had he not been restrained.

As for the extent of his injuries sustained in the car accident, that wasn't so easy to appraise. The muscles in his neck had definitely been strained, cuts seemed to be covering the left side of his face, and his ribs were quite sore. The damage wasn't enough to keep him down, though.

Townes set his jaw tight to absorb the discomfort while he unfolded his rather sore frame. The first thing he did was follow the large-linked chain back to the mounted stud in the rock. The structure he was observing overhead was new, unlike the boulders and land that surrounded him.

He'd seen this place before, but he couldn't put a finger on a where. It had to have been in photographs. He sure as hell would recall if he'd been here in person.

The top edge of the pit was a foot taller than he, but the angle at which he stood allowed him to view a good amount of area from this side of the cavity.

Where the fuck was he?

He had no firearm, no phone, and no wallet. The absence of his phone made it more difficult for Brody to pinpoint his location, but Townes had absolute confidence that he could track the movements from the site of the accident to his current location given enough time.

And that was where the problem lay.

Just how long would Moss keep him alive?

It wasn't that Townes had a death wish, but Moss wasn't the type of sadistic man to just release his prey. That didn't mean that Townes wouldn't put up a hell of a fight. Given any chance at a fair fight, he had no doubt he'd come out the victor. But being in this pit without so much as a weapon to defend himself against the bullet he knew was coming, he was as good as dead.

Where was the sick fuck?

A niggling of doubt crept inside his usual stoic confidence at having made sure Shailyn was untouchable. It would be hard to get through twenty sentries on an extremely well-guarded property that was protected by a state of the art security system to her location. The only way for Moss to get his hands on Shailyn was if she were to willingly leave the property, and his team would never allow that to happen.

Granted, every member of SSI was most likely out in the field tracking his movements, but they wouldn't dare relay anything to Shailyn that would have her do something foolish.

The number of the burner phone she had on her person was programed into his cell phone, but it was listed under another name. That did not mean Moss wouldn't dial each and every number embedded into his contact list. Is that why he wasn't here? Had he gotten ahold of Shailyn and made her believe it was in her best interest to try and leave the estate?

Townes' chest started to tighten at realizing his mistake. Did Moss have enough time to take on such an arduous task? His concern began to accumulate to the point that he was losing sight of what needed to be done.

Sweat began to mix with the blood on the left side of his face. He wiped away the mixture with the back of his hand before starting his search for a weapon. He kept in the back of his mind that he also needed something to work the mount loose from the rock. Upon quick glance, there was nothing to be found for either use.

He pushed aside the concern that wanted to manifest itself into something more and concentrated on the task at hand. He began to test the boulders one by one to see if any were movable. It was a tedious task, but it wasn't like he had anything else to do besides lose his mind…and that wasn't a viable option.

"SHHH," BRETT MURMURED before taking the conversation she was having with Coen on the other side of the white curtain. "We didn't have a choice but to call an ambulance. Her forehead was bleeding, she was having trouble breathing, and she wasn't responding to anything Camryn and I said or did. The emergency doctor believes she had a nervous breakdown and might possibly hurt herself."

Shailyn winced at the layman's term used to diagnose her condition, but there was nothing she could do to correct them. She'd done what she had to do in order to get away from the well-guarded estate. Pressing the phone to her forehead hard enough to break the skin hadn't been pleasant, but it had painted the picture she needed to convey.

All she had to do now was somehow leave this room and arrive at the prearranged meeting spot at the designated time. She peered through her lashes in an attempt to see the large black and white clock behind her. It was futile, but she understood time was slowly ticking away.

Camryn was currently sitting in the chair, talking to Caitlyn on her phone in a low tone. Shailyn truly experienced remorse for misleading them, but she fully believed they would forgive her once they were told all the facts. Right now, it was all she could do not to break down again. She forced her mind to focus and fortify herself for what needed to be done.

Shailyn closed her eyes completely when a nurse entered the small area through the curtain on the opposite side of where Coen and Brett had gone to discuss the current situation. How was she going to slip out without anyone seeing her if no one left her side for any length of time?

Another slice of fear cut through her at the thought of not doing as Moss asked. She had no doubt the consequences would be vile in the worst way, resulting in Townes' death.

She couldn't allow that to happen.

Unfortunately, Coen wasn't the only agent here. Two of the sentries roaming the property had allowed the ambulance onto the property after a thorough search. They then proceeded to follow closely behind in another vehicle and had taken their post on the other side of the curtain. It had certainly caused a commotion for the hospital staff.

"Ma'am, the attending physician has decided that Remy should be admitted for observation," the nurse stated quietly, referring to Shailyn by another name. Brett and Camryn had come up with this tale before dialing 911, deciding it would be safer for everyone involved if Shailyn didn't use her real name. They didn't know that Moss already had the knowledge of her false fatality. "We're waiting for a room to open before we transfer her."

"Thank you," Camryn replied quietly before reiterating what the nurse had conveyed to Caitlyn. She wrapped up the call and opened the curtain slightly so she could share the information with Coen and Brett as the nurse left to check on the room. The soles of her shoes faded into the distance. "They're going to move her…"

Shailyn opened her eyes fully, keeping her gaze trained solely on Camryn's form. She was partially standing outside the curtain, leaving only her backside visible.

There had been a brief moment where Shailyn had made the decision to tell everyone what had happened, but she'd heard the phone call Brett had with Coen. Brody had arrived at the scene to find Townes' firearm and holster lying in the carnage of the crash site. The leather straps had been cut from his body. It was then Shailyn realized they had no idea where Moss had taken Townes.

Shailyn didn't waste time in removing the IV from her arm. She flinched as the needle slid from underneath her skin, but she wasn't left with a choice but to do it herself. She quietly shifted her legs over the gurney as she used a piece of the tape on her arm to stem the flow of blood from the IV site. There was no other choice but to crawl underneath the side curtain into another patient's area. Thankfully, she'd not been asked to change into a hospital gown. She dropped to her hands and knees without hesitation, knowing this would be her only chance.

Adrenaline and fear mixed together, pushing her forward with this foolish purpose of sacrificing herself. Moss might have already killed Townes or might very well kill her upon sight. Either way, she had to try.

She'd weighed the heavy pros and even heavier cons in explaining to Coen what had happened, but all he and the others would have done was try and set up some type of trap to capture Moss. It wouldn't work. It never worked.

She'd thought through her options very carefully, although each had made her physically sick as to what needed to be done. She would roughly have a two-minute lead before Camryn decided to take back her seat and realize that Shailyn was no longer lying in the bed. All hell would break loose, but by then it would be too late.

Would Shailyn have this amount of confidence if she didn't have an ace up her sleeve?

Probably not, but she still would have made the same decision. It was good that she wasn't forced to do this without a lifeline.

Brody had given back her ring this morning. The tracer had been set in place. That act alone would eventually lead the team to her location. She just needed enough time for Moss to take her to wherever he was keeping Townes, so that they both could be rescued before either one of them got hurt.

There were no guarantees, but she had to take that chance.

She truly believed she had no choice but to handle the situation this way. Had she confessed that Moss had reached out to her, they would have kept her secluded away and taken the chance with Townes' life. She couldn't bring herself to allow that to happen.

Shailyn got a few odd looks from patients and their family members as she crawled on her hands and knees to where another patient was waiting to be seen by one of the attending physicians. The twenty-something individual had broken his arm from the way he was holding it against his chest. She mouthed *sorry* as she stood and did her best to appear sane.

"Are you alright, miss?"

"Yes, thank you. I just didn't want to wake my daughter by moving the curtain aside," Shailyn replied softly so that her voice didn't carry. It also justified her quick-thinking response. "You know how children can be. I'm sorry to disturb you."

Shailyn gave a half smile as she moved another curtain aside, still using the backside of the wall so that Coen, Brett, or the two agents who were standing outside her small area wouldn't know she was trying to leave the hospital.

A few more concerned looks and one cubicle with choice words were endured before she reached the last closed-off area near the nurse's station. The bed was thankfully empty. Shailyn recoiled after pulling the curtain aside. A nurse had walked passed the opening, but she thankfully didn't look toward her left.

The double doors caught Shailyn's attention. They were less than eight feet away.

She gave herself a moment to reconsider, knowing all she had to do was tell Coen the truth. They would have her back at the estate and under protection within the hour.

Images of the nightmare she had where Moss held a knife while threatening to slit Townes' throat immediately came to mind. Envisioning the blood spill from his neck propelled her forward. She held her breath as she stepped through the slit in the curtain and quickly walked through the double doors without looking back.

Coen's shouts addressed to the two agents that she was missing from her bed drifted through the closing doors. It was all Shailyn could do but to keep moving forward toward the depths of hell.

HE WAS MERE minutes away from having achieved his goal.

This type of success caused him to be aware of his invincibility. It was truly euphoric.

His fingertips itched with anticipation at the smooth sensation the knife would give him upon sliding the blade through Shailyn's flesh once more.

Hearing Townes' anguish as he could do nothing to stop her pain would only heighten his pleasure.

CHAPTER TWENTY-THREE

T OWNES FORCED HIMSELF to slow his pace as he made a second pass around the circle in hopes to find something that could aid him in escaping this pit of hell. He refused to break and give in to the frustration of being unable to locate anything that could be of use.

Where was Moss?

Had he left Townes here to die?

He wouldn't succeed in that endeavor. Townes would break his own ankle before giving Moss that type of satisfaction.

Someone from the team should be in the area by now. Brody would have had time to retrace movements from the crash site by now. The sun was lowering at a rapid pace, taking with it the humidity that had settled into this circled oven. There was some air movement, but it sure as hell wasn't enough.

Townes wiped away his sweat, grateful that the blood had stopped flowing from his head wounds. He'd removed his dress shirt earlier, pressing on the worst cuts to stop the bleeding. The ribbed tank he'd worn underneath was turning black with dirt from where he'd wiped his hands after attempting to move some of the boulders.

If only he could obtain a large enough piece to try and release these shackles.

Townes lowered himself to the ground, wedging his feet on either side of the mounting fixture. He used part of the shirt that wasn't caked with blood and wiped away the sweat from his hands before he wrapped his fingers around the chain. He leveraged himself so that he was leaning back and using every ounce of strength he had to pull on the links in hopes that some of the screws in the boulder would loosen.

Blood rushed through his ears as he strained every muscle in his body in an effort to achieve triumph. The only thing he succeeded in doing was causing the bump on the side of his head to throb insufferably. He didn't believe he'd gotten the injury during the crash. Moss had most likely rolled his unconscious body into this hellhole. In all honesty, he was lucky to have only received a mild concussion.

"I see you're awake."

Townes thought he'd heard something rustling in the grass while straining over his attempt at loosening the chain from the hardware, so he was somewhat prepared. He casually allowed the soles of his dress shoes to slide away from the rock. He angled his legs so that he could rest his arms over his knees, emanating a casual air of indifference.

Moss fed off fear.

"That I am," Townes said, not bothering to seek out Moss' position. The sound of his voice would do that for him. "I've got to hand it to you, Moss. I wasn't expecting you to lose patience so easily to bring this game to a close."

"Is that what you think?"

Moss' probing question set Townes on edge, though he did his best not to show his unease. He feigned wiping away a smudge on his shoe to buy a little more time. This was all a battle of wits, nothing more.

"Well, we discovered the body you left in the ruins of that

cabin was your twin brother. I'm relatively sure you weren't expecting us to connect the dots so easily. I can't imagine how hard it was for your mother to keep him locked up on the farm," Townes commiserated wryly. He figured now was the point in which he could push back with assumptions that would either get him killed quickly or give the team more time to find his location. "I've been wondering something, though. Were you the one who blinded him? Caroline Marinovic somehow found out about him, didn't she? Did you sneak him into the diner one day? Did Caroline favor him over you?"

The painful whimper that drifted over the opening of the pit sliced fear through Townes in a manner he never experienced before. He was on his feet before his mind could warn him he was playing into Moss' hands, but instinct to stop Shailyn from being hurt even worse than before was too strong.

What the hell was she doing here?

"Let her go, Moss." Had Townes had access to a machete, he would have hacked his own leg off in a matter of minutes to finish what should have ended years ago. "I *will* kill you. Do you understand that?"

Moss was staring at Townes in abject fury. His speculation on the connection between Caroline and Moss had been confirmed, though it took him a second to process that information. He was too busy looking over Shailyn to ensure she hadn't been hurt in any way.

There was a plea in her emerald green eyes for forgiveness. It was then he realized she'd purposefully put herself into the hands of Moss. She'd done so to save Townes' life. His gut twisted at the sacrifice she'd made, because all would be for naught.

Damn it.

He'd done everything in his power to give Shailyn her life

back. Moss would now kill them both, but not before he enjoyed serving both of them up a bit of torture.

"You're talking about something you know nothing about," Moss exclaimed after he'd gathered his composure. He then ran a hand over Shailyn's auburn hair as if she were nothing but a mere doll. The way she closed her eyes made it obvious she was doing her best not lose the contents of her stomach. "All that really matters is that Shailyn is back with me. I've waited a long time for this moment."

He tensed at Moss' implication. He was going to force Townes to hear every scream of pain that fell from her lips. Nausea took hold, but he pushed it back as he made every effort to delay the inevitable.

Where was his team? How in the hell had Moss gotten his hooks into Shailyn?

"Really?" Townes taunted, hoping he wasn't making a mistake. Moss would surely see through his attempt at wasting time. He was too intelligent to fall for it unless Townes could find something that shook the monster at his core. "I figured you would have rather spent more time with your brother, considering it was him who took Caroline Marinovic away from you."

Moss stared down into the pit through his rimless glasses that had been a staple of his features since he was in his teens. A flush of anger rose in his face just as quick as his step forward, giving Townes exactly what he wanted.

"Are you surprised that I could figure out what happened all those years ago, Moss?"

Townes purposefully shook his head in disappointment, catching Shailyn's expression as she followed the chain around his ankle to the stone wall. He needed her to leave him here while she sought some type of safety. He still wasn't sure how Moss got to Shailyn, but it was more than apparent that she'd come with him on her own free will. Her hands and feet weren't secured.

"You left us with DNA that closely resembled yours, you went back to where Caroline had originally been buried, and you allowed Lucas Grove to live after the fact." Townes *tsked* his displeasure, knowing full well that Moss would take the gesture as an insult. "You're so incredibly easy to read, Moss."

Townes immediately stepped forward and closed his hands into tight fists when Moss all but dragged Shailyn away from the side of the pit. The chain's rattling wasn't loud enough to drown out Shailyn's protests.

He pressed his fists to his eyes as he struggled to figure out how to stop Moss from doing to Shailyn what she'd already experienced under his hand and what she saw in her nightmares every fucking night.

This was his nightmare.

How had they come to be here?

"Moss!" Townes understood that he was giving Moss what he wanted, but desperation was clawing at his chest. It was becoming harder and harder to breathe the longer Shailyn was out of his line of vision. "Did Caroline beg you to save her from your brother? Did being hidden and locked away cause your brother to go insane? Or was he jealous of Caroline? Did she blame you for dragging her into your family full of psychopaths?"

Townes could very well be off the mark, but he fully believed from Moss' initial reaction that his brother had killed Caroline Marinovic. Had she gone looking for him only to find him involved with something illegal? Had he killed her to prove a point, or had he been just as fucked up in the head as Moss?

The team had gotten this lead a little too late.

"He showed me who I truly was." Moss finally appeared on

the right side of the pit, but he was without Shailyn. Where was she? The sun was setting, so it was becoming harder to see Moss' facial expressions. His tone suggested he was calmer than before. That wasn't what Townes had been going for and another wave of desperation hit. "Alexander showed me my true calling."

Townes understood where he went wrong. Caroline might have begged Moss to help her in her time of need, but her pleas had somehow stirred that twisted, sadistic part of his soul.

It was the moment he became a killer himself.

"Tell me one thing before you begin whatever is you're going to do," Townes asked, sparing Shailyn only a few more moments of peace. He had to swallow in order to get the words out. "How did you find her?"

It wasn't dark enough yet to hide Moss' vile smile. Was that the hideous leer Shailyn had seen every time Moss slid the blade into her flesh? The urge to wrap his hands around Moss' throat and squeeze the life out of him was overwhelming, but he was helpless chained to this wall.

Anguish clawed at the back of his throat.

"You have no parents, no siblings, and the contact list on your phone is filled with law enforcement names." Moss pushed his rimmed glasses higher up on the bridge of his nose. It was as if he wanted to see Townes' reaction clearly for his own enjoyment. "It didn't take me long to have a friend of mine run the names. Only one stood out as a false flag."

Townes would have continued to ask questions or done anything to delay the inevitable, but something caught Moss' attention. He immediately disappeared. Being in this shallow crater made it hard to catch sounds that were in the distance. Townes remained still and held his breath in an attempt to hear what could be happening.

Had the team finally arrived? Had Brody been able to retrace Moss' steps from the scene of the accident? Those details were still vague, because there was no way in hell Moss could have been directly involved. He didn't have a scratch on him to indicate he'd been in one of the vehicles.

"No!"

Shailyn's scream resonated through the air. Horrible images flashed vividly through Townes' mind as to the torture Moss was inflicting upon her.

"God, no." Townes words were strangled, but that didn't stop him from planting a foot on the stone where the chain was mounted. He pulled with all his might, straining every muscle in his body in an attempt at freedom. "Moooosssss!"

CHAPTER TWENTY-FOUR

S HAILYN SAGGED WITH relief upon hearing the faint sound of multiple, fast-moving vehicles approaching. She twisted against the stone pillar Moss had shackled her to in order to pick up where he'd left off all those years ago, but she couldn't make out any headlights. Doubt crept up her spine that the vehicles didn't belong to the team. What if it was someone here to help Moss carry out his ritual blood sacrifice?

He'd driven her out to what she now recalled being the New Smyrna Old Sugar Mills. It was a deserted plantation where the mill had been left abandoned in 1835 after a raid by the Seminoles caused by tensions that had been stirring between them, the settlers, and the U.S. government.

This place had been left abandoned. It was the perfect location for what Moss intended to carry out this evening.

Would Brody reach them in time?

She'd followed every detail Moss had given her with precision. Her legs had almost given out a couple of times in doubt and fear as she walked to the designated meeting area. Questions had haunted her with every step she took.

What if she'd made the wrong decision?

What if Brody wasn't able to access the signal on the transmitter he'd placed in her ring? He said all he needed was a phone of any type to transmit the signal to the service provider. Moss had one in his possession, but would it still work?

Leaving the hospital without being seen hadn't been easy, but she'd done it with success. Moss had been waiting for her a half mile away on the corner of a busy intersection.

She would have recognized the build of his body anywhere.

Nausea had clamped down on her stomach with a vengeance. Moss was standing in broad daylight as men, women, and children walked around him without even a hint of who they were brushing past to get to their destinations. They were clueless, even if he had been wearing a ball cap pulled low on his forehead. Could they not sense the evil emanating from this monster among them?

Moss held himself in an almost unnaturally straight position, so unlike now as he was rapidly moving in her direction. He'd pulled out the knife that had been in his possession the entire car ride here and pointed the tip directly at her as he advanced.

"No!"

Shailyn tried to cover her face, but the zip ties around her wrists held her hands securely behind her back. All she could manage was to turn her head away at the attack.

Moss took her by surprise when he dragged her toward the large opening in the ground once more. She hadn't attempted to run for several reasons. One of them was her ring would lead the team here to this exact location, and the other was Townes. She would never leave him…even if doing so resulted in her death.

The only other motivation keeping her here was to watch Moss die at the hands of SSI. The team was somewhere close by or otherwise Moss wouldn't be panicking.

She'd outsmarted him.

Before any satisfaction could chase away her rooted fear, he spun her around to face him. His beady little eyes let her know that he wasn't rattled in the least by this interruption. It was then that terror filled every core of her being.

With a sneer of contempt at being placed in this no-win situation, he shoved her backward into the darkening pit. Why was it that she was so focused on the setting sun? She didn't want to die. She certainly didn't want to die in the dark.

But she would be able to do anything in Townes' arms.

Shailyn was weightless as she soared in the air, gravity immediately taking hold and sucking her down inside the void. Oddly enough, it was in that moment she realized that she was a different woman than the one who'd been so innocent so long ago.

Moss might take her life tonight, but she'd lived more in this last week than in all the years he'd stolen from her. Townes had given her that gift.

It was also he who caught her in his arms as he broke her fall with his body. Her momentum knocked him backward, but the chain prevented him from being fully able to shield her upper body. The impact of the hard ground stole the air from her lungs, making it impossible to scream as her hair was yanked, all but forcing her back to her feet.

Shailyn wasn't able to stop Moss from tearing her away from Townes, mostly due to the fact that her hands were still bound behind her. The hard plastic was digging into her skin as a reminder that she was still at Moss' mercy. He held her tight against his chest with a knife at her throat.

"It's over, Moss. Drop your weapon or I'll shoot."

Shailyn didn't bother looking up at the sound of Brody's declaration. She sought Townes' gaze, needing him to know she was okay with however this played out. No matter what happened from this point on…he would be alive come tomorrow morning.

"You heard him." Townes had managed to get to his feet, regardless that the shackle around his lower leg prevented him from coming any closer. Not even being chained to a wall could take away his virility. "It's over, Moss."

Shailyn hadn't expected the sharp tip of a knife to enter her left side. The blade easily sliced through the material of her shirt and her sensitive flesh. She arched against the searing pain, unable to stop her scream from piercing the air or the sweat from beading on her skin.

"Take the fucking shot!"

Moss' foul laughter filled the air, but it barely cut through the blood rushing in her ears. He drew the knife out, reminding her of their previous time together. She was finally able to breathe. Where had he gotten a second knife? One was already at her throat, preventing her from escaping.

"I-I'm okay," Shailyn managed to say, all the while tensing to receive another wound. She recalled how often Moss liked to hear her scream. Her nightmare wasn't over, but her presence kept Moss from hurting Townes. "Just do it, Brody. It's alright."

Townes might have ordered Brody or one of the other team members to shoot Moss, but his slight frame allowed him to use her as an effective shield. He was literally hiding behind her in a manner that wouldn't allow him to be targeted. They would have to shoot her first. It was doubtful the team would end this standoff in such a manner.

It wouldn't matter if she bled out first.

"Moss, what's the point in all this?" It was obvious that Townes was trying to take Moss' attention off her, but it was futile effort. Shailyn bit her lip to keep from crying out as the blade once again tore into her flesh. "Do you want the headlines to read that you died because I outsmarted you once again?"

Shailyn's strangled cry was cut short when the blade was

ripped out of her back. The hot, burning sensation gave way to the fact that she was bleeding rather profusely, but she managed to keep her knees locked together. She didn't want the knife at her throat to slip.

"I have always been prepared to die, Townes Calvert." Moss' breath was hot against her hair, the disgusting warmth seeping through the strands. He could very well keep stabbing her until she bled out during this standoff. There was nothing stopping him from doing so unless one of the team members ended this nightmare. "I hadn't wished it so soon, but I'll be happy to take Shailyn with me to the afterlife. You are right about my sweet Caroline, though. No one has ever come close to giving me that initial pleasure of hearing those rewarding screams. Of course, Shailyn was pure gold all those years ago. She still *is* pure gold."

Shailyn expected the slice of the blade this time, unable to stop herself from arching away from the unavoidable tip. It broke the skin the same moment a gunshot was discharged from above. She waited for the searing pain to bloom either in her chest or head, but nothing happened.

Darkness had fallen quickly. The sudden quiet had her frantically searching for Townes' comforting grey stare for answers, but dusk made that almost impossible. She couldn't make out his features in the obscure shadows.

Light unexpectedly blinded her and she involuntarily lowered her face. She flinched, knowing the sharp edge of the knife would no doubt cut her throat. A warmer sensation started to heat her hair and skin. She'd been shot in the neck. She braced herself for the pain.

Oh, my God.

"Someone get her away from him!" Townes ordered harshly, the rattling of the chain breaking through the low hum in her ears. "Now! And get some bolt cutters!"

The knife at her throat fell away as Moss crumpled at her feet, sending her staggering forward. Townes had his arms outstretched, but nothing was making sense as she tried to assimilate what had taken place. She slowly turned to find Moss' body lying on the ground at an awkward angle. She was so used to seeing his wire-rimmed glasses that she immediately noticed they were missing.

Blood pooled down what was left of Moss' features. His sightless gaze appeared slightly surprised at meeting death.

He hadn't been ready.

"Shailyn, look at me." Sawyer was suddenly standing in front of her, blocking her view of something she wished had happened for years. "The paramedics are on their way. I need you to sit down so that we can put pressure on those wounds."

Shailyn wasn't sure why it was so hard to answer him. It was more than apparent that she wasn't the one shot, but everything around her seemed to be happening to someone else. Her hands were suddenly free and by her sides.

"We need more light down here!" Coen called up to someone as he and Sawyer all but forced her to the ground. They'd done so in a manner that had her facing away from what was left of the man who had haunted her every minute of every day. "And where are those bolt cutters?"

"Freckles," Townes called to her softly. It was a wonder she'd even heard him over the shouting of the others. "Freckles, it's over. It's all over."

Shailyn finally set eyes on the man she'd lived far too long without. His dark brown hair hung around his face, covering the scar that she'd found so endearing. It shouted that he was merely human, yet he was the one who had orchestrated this manhunt. Granted, it hadn't gone the way anyone had ever imagined, but he was right…it was over.

She leaned forward on her hands and knees, slowly crawling over to where he'd lowered himself to the ground. He was still hindered by the chain. She ignored Sawyer and Coen's calls of concern as she finally reached her destination.

Townes all but dragged her into his embrace, holding onto her as if Moss might come back to life and take her away. He didn't care that the very blood and brain matter of the man who'd made their lives hell was all over the back of her. Neither did she.

All the stains left behind could be washed away.

They sat on the ground as the chaos around them continued, safe in one another's arms. There was no need for words. There was no need for tears.

They savored the bright future awaiting them both that had nothing to do with the artificial light shining down on them from above.

CHAPTER TWENTY-FIVE

C HRISTMAS MORNING DAWNED two days later, bringing with it sunshine that came through the shutters. Its brightness had nothing on the colorful lights strewn around the Christmas tree or the vibrant wrapping paper that littered the floor. The only thing to give the brilliance any competition was Brody's new Hawaiian shirts. Lord, they were loud.

"Why do you keep you looking over at Brody?" Shailyn asked, tilting her head up to receive an answer. She radiated happiness, regardless that the stitches in her side and back had to be sore. Her smile faded somewhat at his silence. "Has something happened with the investigation?"

Townes had stayed by her side for the past thirty-six hours, allowing the team to handle the remaining holes of the investigation. The other victim in the car accident that had given Moss an opportunity to drag Townes away had been one of his followers from way back when he was serving his sentence. The woman was now in custody, but she would most likely end up in front of a jury after her stint in the hospital. Her lawyer was claiming insanity. He sure as hell wasn't wrong about that. She was crazy as a loon. Her condition turned for the worse when she received word that Moss had been gunned down and was roasting in hell.

"No," Townes replied, stroking her arm in reassurance. He

motioned that she should eat the blueberry muffin Brett had made at an ungodly hour of the morning to signify that it was Christmas morning. "Eat. You're going to need your stamina when your parents come to visit."

Shailyn pursed her lips, telling him that she didn't believe his denial. He shot another look Brody's way, but the man shook his head in answer to Townes' silent question.

His Christmas present for Shailyn had yet to arrive. It was supposed to have been delivered thirty minutes ago, but no vehicle had approached the perimeter as of yet. There were still around ten sentries roaming the property, but that had more to do with the media than anything. He would gradually take that number down to five or so, always having the men and women on hand in case an acolyte decided to show up and try to finish what Moss started.

"Here," Sawyer called out, reaching for a rectangular box wrapped in silver and white paper. It was complemented by a rather large silver bow. "Calvert. This one is for you."

He frowned, wondering what the team was up to now. Everyone had opened their presents, though this year was rather sparse considering the amount of time they'd spent away from home.

"Put it back under the tree," Townes demanded with a wave of his hand. "It probably contains the receipt for the bonus Brody gave himself for the additional admin work he's been doing, and this is how he's breaking it to me."

"Oh, that money is already in my bank account," Brody countered with a laugh. He rubbed his fingers together to indicate the large amount. "And I also gave myself hazard pay since my ass isn't supposed to be in the field. Thank you, Calvert, for your overwhelming generosity."

Townes muttered a few choice words before leaning forward

and taking the proffered gift. Shailyn had set aside her blueberry muffin. It needed butter, anyway.

She was now watching him a little too intently. That made him suspect this gift was from her. He recalled her doing some online shopping with the other women, but he thought those gifts were for her parents. As a matter of fact, those two boxes were wrapped and still tucked underneath the tree somewhere.

"You realize that you're going to be buying the donuts for the entire month of January, right?" Royce said with a smile, rubbing in the fact that he'd been purposefully buying only one of a particular kind of donut and letting Keane and Brody fight over it. "Keane, looks like you're shit out of luck."

Keane shot Brody the bird before closing the lid on the new watch Ashlyn had gotten him for Christmas. Everyone had pretty much already exchanged gifts, even Remy's special present to Brody. She'd gotten him an autographed Hawaiian shirt worn by Tom Selleck himself during the show's eight-season run.

It only served to remind Townes that Shailyn's gift hadn't arrived on time this morning.

"Townes?" Shailyn's hand rested gently on his. Her softening gaze made him realize this present was from her. His chest tightened with emotion as he glanced down at the silver and white present wrapped so perfectly. He wanted to savor this moment. "Merry Christmas."

Those two sweet words had almost been stolen from them.

"Please, Townes, open it."

He slid a finger under one of the corners, the tape tearing away from the wrapping paper instantly. The heat from everyone's gazes were on him, but he didn't mind. These men and women were his family. There was much more to be said regarding loyalty than blood.

The bow and paper slid to the ground. In his hand was a

white box. He slowly lifted the lid and shifted aside the silver tissue paper. His throat constricted at what lay inside. He recognized the hard-crafted work carved into the wood. He should. The man had constructed the house they all sat in to celebrate this Christmas.

Home.

The word wasn't alone. Underneath, it listed Shailyn's and his names…as well as the entire team.

"Thank you, freckles," Townes managed to say around the constriction of his throat. "We'll hang it up on the front porch today."

Townes brushed his fingers over her cheek, staring into those emerald green eyes that now held the sparkle he'd so longed to see. He pressed his lips to hers, ignoring the applause from the surrounding group.

"Calvert, you're up."

Brody's declaration had Townes carefully setting aside his present so that he could guide Shailyn outside. Everyone fell in line, not wanting to miss out on what was about to happen.

The coolness of the morning wasn't enough to warrant sweaters or jackets due to the warm sunshine. The sound of a vehicle broke through the American Elm trees lining the long, private lane. A large white van finally broke in the clearing past the guard shack.

"What did you do?" Shailyn asked with a laugh, following Townes down the wooden stairs.

Townes remained silent, allowing the driver to put the van in park before exiting. He got out of the vehicle with a smile, understanding that this had been kept a secret. He opened the back doors.

Out came a bundle of fur in the form of a yellow Labrador Retriever. The red bow around her neck signified she was the one chosen for Shailyn. The driver started walking forward with the excited puppy in his arms.

"Townes?" Shailyn whispered in awe, covering her lips with her hands. She quickly turned and lifted herself up on her tiptoes to wrap her arms around his neck. He leaned down to make it easier for her, not wanting her stitches to pull. "He's mine?"

"*She* is yours," Townes corrected, pressing his forehead against hers. There was something he needed her to know. "Unconditional love comes in many forms, Shailyn. Mine included."

"I love you, too, Townes Calvert. With all my heart."

The driver closed the distance, causing Shailyn to turn and take the bundle of joy from his arms. The puppy licked her chin and cheeks excitedly, wagging her tail as if she understood this was her new home. Shailyn held onto the little furbaby with a smile that rivaled the sun. Her laugh rang out when everyone closed in to meet the new member of the family.

"Merry Christmas, freckles."

~ The End ~

Thank you for reading Deadly Premonitions and joining me in the conclusion of the Safeguard Series!

I hope that you'll love the Kendall family—coming in January 2018—as much as you loved the SSI team members.

You can read all about the Keys to Love series below and can also preorder your copies HERE
kennedylayne.com/keys-to-love-book-one-mdash-unlocking-fear.html

Books by Kennedy Layne

Surviving Ashes Series

Essential Beginnings (Surviving Ashes, Book One)
Hidden Ashes (Surviving Ashes, Book Two)
Buried Flames (Surviving Ashes, Book Three)
Endless Flames (Surviving Ashes, Book Four)
Rising Flames (Surviving Ashes, Book Five)

CSA Case Files Series

Captured Innocence (CSA Case Files 1)
Sinful Resurrection (CSA Case Files 2)
Renewed Faith (CSA Case Files 3)
Campaign of Desire (CSA Case Files 4)
Internal Temptation (CSA Case Files 5)
Radiant Surrender (CSA Case Files 6)
Redeem My Heart (CSA Case Files 7)

Red Starr Series

Starr's Awakening & Hearths of Fire (Red Starr, Book One)
Targets Entangled (Red Starr, Book Two)
Igniting Passion (Red Starr, Book Three)
Untold Devotion (Red Starr, Book Four)
Fulfilling Promises (Red Starr, Book Five)
Fated Identity (Red Starr, Book Six)
Red's Salvation (Red Starr, Book Seven)

The Safeguard Series

Brutal Obsession (The Safeguard Series, Book One)
Faithful Addiction (The Safeguard Series, Book Two)
Distant Illusions (The Safeguard Series, Book Three)
Casual Impressions (The Safeguard Series, Book Four)
Honest Intentions (The Safeguard Series, Book Five)
Deadly Premonitions (The Safeguard Series, Book Six)

About the Author

First and foremost, I love life. I love that I'm a wife, mother, daughter, sister… and a writer.

I am one of the lucky women in this world who gets to do what makes them happy. As long as I have a cup of coffee (maybe two or three) and my laptop, the stories evolve themselves and I try to do them justice. I draw my inspiration from a retired Marine Master Sergeant that swept me off of my feet and has drawn me into a world that fulfills all of my deepest and darkest desires. Erotic romance, military men, intrigue, with a little bit of kinky chili pepper (his recipe), fill my head and there is nothing more satisfying than making the hero and heroine fulfill their destinies.

Thank you for having joined me on their journeys…

Email:

kennedylayneauthor@gmail.com

Facebook:

facebook.com/kennedy.layne.94

Twitter:

twitter.com/KennedyL_Author

Website:

www.kennedylayne.com

Newsletter:

www.kennedylayne.com/newsletter.html

CPSIA information can be obtained
at www.ICGtesting.com
Printed in the USA
LVOW07s1624161117
556556LV00001B/170/P